MW01273381

I got a girl and Ruby is her name
She don't love me but I love her just the same
Ruby Baby, how I want you
Like a ghost I'm gonna haunt you
Ruby Baby, when will you be mine?

Ruby Ruby

(A MURDER MYSTERY)

BRADLEY HARRIS

ANVIL PRESS PUBLISHERS

Printed and bound in Canada
First Edition
Cover Design: Levita Design

CANADIAN CATALOGUING IN PUBLICATION DATA

Harris, Bradley 1952-
Ruby ruby

ISBN 1-895636-23-X

I. Title
PS8565.A64817R82 1999   C813'.54   C99-910328-8
PR9199.3.H34585R82 1999

Represented in Canada by the Literary Press Group
Distributed by General Distribution Services

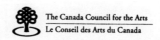

Anvil Press
Suite 204-A 175 East Broadway,
Vancouver, B.C. V5T 1W2 CANADA

Acknowledgements:

I am grateful for the assistance of The Canada Council for the Arts in the publication and promotion of *Ruby Ruby*.

Brian Kaufman and Johanne Provencal of Anvil Press deserve much praise for their professionalism; they're pros with a sense of humour.

My Canadian family—Ed and Kay Harris, sibs Murray, Malcolm, and Laurie, Barb Harris, Merle Woods, Kathryn Woods and Graham Woods—have shown a love and patience beyond my capacity to thank, and beyond deserving.

Canadian friends—Norma Duke, Craig Cope, Doug Levis, Bob Sinden, Gary Lowe, Vicky Georgijevic, Laurence Chrismas, Kevin Jordan, Gael Spivak, Tom Phillips and others—will find their voices in *Ruby Ruby* and works to follow. So will American friends—Cliff Laird, Mark Mayhall, Mike Peterson, Mike Corley, Mike Nickel and Paul Craig among them.

My American family—urchins Jon, Dave, and Chris, outlaw parental units Bee and Paul Fritsche, have been patient and generous. Trish, my beloved, supports the arts with more than even the Canada Council has ever contemplated, or any applicant ever asked.

Thanks to those who taught me to write: Bill Washburn, Kai Nielsen, Rosemary Nixon, Cecelia Frey, Aritha Van Herk, Jo McDougall, Tom Russell, Rick DeMarinis, John Bensko, Stephen Malin, Brett Singer. Thanks are also due many in and around American English lit., ESL, linguistics and cre-ative writing: Teresa Dalle (a superb professor, mentor, and friend, and the only woman other than my mother and my wife ever to have spat on a kleenex to wipe my cheek), Emily Thrush, Debbie Hunt, Reginald Dalle, Eric Dalle, Paul Naylor, Bruce Speck, Guy Bailey, Jan Tillery, Edgar Schneider, Eric Chandler, Susan Scheckel (than whom no greater teacher can be thought), Mary C. Berni, Necie-Elizabeth Young, Tami Taylor, Merlin Taylor, Kristin Costeck, Laura Sullivan, Mary

Battle, Charles Hall, Brian Isbell, Angela Hoehn, Robin
Towne, Susan Fitzgerald, Charles O'Bryant, Marvin Ching,
Joan Weatherly, Mickie Ryan and Tommie Tracy.

There are more to thank. There's much more to be grateful
for. I'm just praying for another novel, another page of
acknowledgements in which to do it.

Bradley Harris
Expatriate Canadian
Memphis, Tennessee
July, 1999

p.s. Oh, yes. And of course Peg Oneil, without whom,
etcetera, etcetera . . .

FOR MY BELOVED TRISH

≈ ≈ ≈

The car, dark, pulls up on the street outside Green's Lounge, ignores a sign not to park in the driveway. Two figures get out. Suits. Black man. White man. A line extends outside the door. The blues, loud but dulled when the door is shut, loud and acute, as guitar riffs sharp and bent, wail on the high frets and whine whiskey-tight when the door opens wide to let someone out. The line shifts aside. The man checking weapons at the door just nods. The men tour both rooms before leaving. They slide, the black man first, between the bodies and through the shout and the smoke. They are oblivious to the music, though the sax man sees through stylish shades, seems to watch them as he plays a run of riffs, then the guitar, climbing to the short, screaming frets where the fingers are almost too fat to work the strings.

≈ ≈ ≈

CHAPTER 1

As I drove all the way in from Germantown along the fifteen-mile spine of Poplar Avenue, that crap about a red sky at morning ran through my head, started nibbling at the edge of my sanity about the same time as the thought of pulling into the Circle K on Cooper for some coffee. It seemed irreverent, but what the hell—there was no night left anyway for whoever it was we'd had on duty, and by the time I got back to Lynette I'd be—at best—just in time to catch a shower and church. I ran the phone call back through my mind.

Christ, I'd said, and that, more than the call from dispatch, had woken Lynette.

What do you mean—'incident'?

Honey, what's wrong?

There's nothing wrong.

Jack?

It's all right, it's all right, Lynette, go back to—

Who is it, Jack?

Okay, I'll drive right in—

Honey? Who is it?

And I said again, *Christ. I don't even know.*

Lamont, Lamont, Lamont Franklin. I'd said the name Lamont a hundred times in my head all the way in along Poplar and along Central to Cooper, trying to see if I knew the guy as more than a name from a file. But the Company has thirteen- to fourteen-hundred people in the field or on standby at any given time. Franklin's a common name in Memphis, common everywhere in The Delta. We must have had twenty on the rolls, and I couldn't get a fix, the name was *wrong*, somehow. Till it hit me.

Listen, this is Memphis. You get used to certain things, certain ideas, certain patterns. "That's the way it is." Lord, I used to despise that phrase, used to laugh at it, ridicule it, when I first came to the MidSouth. The last three, four years, I'd begun hearing it from my own lips, straight. After a while—no matter that you're a nice, liberal, milk-drinking, hockey-playing, whole-wheat Canuck from Saskatoon or not—somebody buys a pack of Newports, a quart can of Colt 45 in a brown paper bag, says *Mm-hmm I know that's right*, and carries a name like Lamont Franklin, he's black, that's all there is to it, and that you can bet the kiddies' college money on. That's the way it is. I hate that saying. That's the way it is has been the official Southern National Excuse since the Reconstruction. It used to be the kind of thing I couldn't even bring myself to say, that I'd call somebody on if they said it. And now—ah, shit.

In a hard rush as I crossed the Parkway on Central, it came to me—my fix. *Monty.* Monty Franklin. He was just 'Monty' to most everybody—nobody ever used his last name. Monty was what you'd get from central

11

casting if you asked for a night watchman: a sixty-something white guy, a little short, a little round, a Floyd-the-barber moustache, rarely a smile when he's working. Plodding, methodical, by the book, takes it all maybe a wee bit too seriously. The kind of security guard who actually cleaned his gun. I never knew him well. Monty had been with the Company for years, a good ten before I'd come on board in '88. He'd been way down in South Memphis at the Defense Depot on Airways, since the day he'd come back from Korea, most of that time as an Ordnance Corps master sergeant, then a civilian employee with National Defense, then with us when the Company took over the Depot's perimeter security contract. That was just before I came to Memphis. Monty had taken this latest assignment in Midtown only because he and his wife had lived the best part of their married life in the Cooper-Young area and he could walk home from work.

One summer on a hot, wet Friday afternoon, Lynette had talked me into enduring one of those god-awful toothpick, cheese, white-wine, abstract-inhibitionist openings at some upstart gallery just off Young, and, afterward, spotting him walking to work along Cooper Street, lunch pail and all, we'd stopped to offer him a lift. Nice guy, to be sure. But stiff. *Yes, sir. Thank you, sir.* And his trademark: *Tickety-boo, sir.* I'd asked him to call me Jack—everybody does: I don't really believe in rank much anymore. But he never did, save the first time, when it sounded forced. And Monty wouldn't go near any kind of real familiarity with my wife. He called her *Miz Lynette*—that's Southern for: *I'd like to call you by your first name, ma'am, but I can't.*

Lynette and I had got used to seeing the two of them at most of the Company's social events— Christmas, the Memphis-in-May Barbecue Dance, the Dead-Elvis Week do, and what-not. The two of them would walk in, her arm tucked under his. He'd hold her chair while she settled herself, and Monty would stand and nervously smooth his jacket front anytime any woman came near or left. She was old, his wife, but she was pretty in a pale, Irish-lace kind of way. And small, smaller than him. Her smile was modest and fragile and from another time. She had one of those feminine names no one else has but you can't quite remember—Clara, Clarisse, Camille—and Lynette would touch my elbow and smile and say, *Aren't they darling?* as they danced. Now here I was, sipping bad, tepid coffee from a styrofoam cup, standing in a parking lot outside an empty factory, watching this man's blood dry where it had gurgled out of his throat and trickled in a wandering rill of red across the asphalt and down a drain in the driveway.

"Hey! Who're you?" The voice had more than a little edge. I turned. I was about to answer—attitude notwithstanding—when Jimmy Page stepped in. Jimmy looked a lot like George Foreman and was a damn sight more likely to listen to Lightnin' Hopkins than to his English-rocker namesake. Jimmy nodded, shook my hand, and introduced me to the attitude. "Gordon MacDonald. Second Shift. Homicide,"

Jimmy said, and he added, "Lieutenant MacDonald is a *new* boy," with a nod to me. "New in the rank, anyways," he said. He got a cold glance from MacDonald, then grinned in reply. "Gordo here's been coming up some time now, under my own brilliant tutelage." Jimmy slapped the man's back. MacDonald didn't like it. Jimmy just smiled, and his hands ran, thumb and forefinger, symmetrically down the lapels of his suit.

MacDonald was a small guy, seemed about half Jimmy's size, a compact, tight man, except for a slight paunch that was just a jot shy of straining the buttons of his fitted shirt. Around thirty-five, shaven head, in a suit way too good for a cop. Too *tasteful*, the thought occurred to me before I recoiled from it. MacDonald didn't smile, but he didn't take his eyes off me either. No matter how much I read up on the history, on the wayward and sometimes vicious ways of my Scots forebears, in what they did in their conquered and conquering land and abroad with swords and rifles and names—and I am sorry for this, I truly am—I had, and I still do have, some vague kind of trouble with the notion of MacDonald as a name for black people. Not that I don't like it, it's just that I can't quite get accustomed to it. And, from the looks of things, MacDonald had some vague kind of trouble with me as well.

"Gordon, meet Mr. Jack Minyard. Jack, here, is Chief of Security Operations and Personnel with Marksman Security." MacDonald stuck out his hand to take mine but he eyed me with something between a generic contempt for civilians and a more personal feeling that I just couldn't put my finger on. "Be nice to the man, Gordo," Jimmy said. "Half the force, half your unit included, moonlights for Marksman Security thanks to the fabulous wages and perks furnished by Mayor Willie and the good taxpayers of Memphis." MacDonald nodded, is all, dead cold, and he glanced my way and disappeared to talk to a uniform over by the guardhouse where two white-overalled guys from MidSouth Body Removal shuffled, hands in pockets, waiting for the police photographer to finish.

"I never had a chance to tell you, Jimmy. Congratulations." I hadn't seen him since he'd been promoted to major a few months back, and I wanted to get it in, even if we were in the middle of a murder scene, so I just said it. Memphis P.D. is one of the few forces you'll find that even has the rank of major, and the reason is, as much as anything, that Memphis P.D. is just plain fat with officer ranks and way too thin on the ground. I'd never made it past captain. The fact I'd never held the rank of major myself except on an acting basis—different line of work, different country notwithstanding—gave me the oddest twinge of jealousy.

"Thanks," he said, but he got right down to it. "What the hell's *in* this building, Jack?"

"Nothing," I said. "The place is empty. Totally empty. I don't even know whether we have keys for the building, to tell you the truth. Got a guy back at the office on it. Used to be a pie factory, the old days, till the county health people couldn't look the other way anymore and the place got condemned. Then it was used as a warehouse for awhile, back in the seventies. There's been nothing here for years, far as I'm aware."

"Then why a security guard at all?"

I had to admit I didn't know. Jimmy pointed out the obvious. "Look. Chain-link fence, a good seven or eight feet high. Three-strand outward overhang. Concertina wire, for God's—" Jimmy held out his hand for a sip of my coffee.

"Shit, I don't know, Jimmy. I'll look up the contract when I get to the office, okay?"

"Shit is right." Jimmy handed the cup back.

"Any ideas?" I asked.

"Tell you, Jack," he said. "On average, we've got a homicide every one-point-two days in Memphis. I barely got a God damn *list,* let alone an idea."

"So what's the deal? Robbery? Gang thing? What? How'd they break in, Jimmy?"

"I was just wonderin' if you could shed some light on that, Jack," he said. I wondered at the *wonderin'*— Jimmy generally was given to hyper-correction more than a lot of English professors I knew; like more than a few people you'll meet in Memphis, he was consciously fastidious about not 'talkin' Southern.' By which he meant, people said: talkin' black. "You see, Jack, they didn't break in at all. Your man's lying dead outside his guardhouse, the guardhouse is what—fifty, sixty yards inside the fence. Now you know God damn well the sumbitches didn't pole-vault over that fence. And not only that, but you go take you a look-see—the padlock's on the fence gate, locked, and the key's still on his belt."

"So he let them—let whoever it was—in."

"Looks like." Jimmy gave me a you-figure-it-out look.

"And what? What's your theory, Jimmy? Huh? You're thinking whoever it was let himself out the gate and locked the padlock behind him? With their own key?"

"That's my theory, Jack, yeah. You got a better one?"

A voice across the lot. "We'll need his file, of course. His personnel file." MacDonald again. He looked at me expectantly.

"It's Sunday morning, Gordo," Jimmy said. "Come on. Tomorrow morning'll be soon enough, okay?" MacDonald started to speak, but Jimmy just looked at him till MacDonald left again, then Jimmy turned to me.

I doubted the answer would be in that file, whatever the question was, and I said so. I remembered I'd been into the file myself a few months back. I'd been reviewing nominations for the company's Guardsman of the Year Award, and I'd gone through a foot-high stack of individual personnel files Arlene had given me, the ones with the yellow stickies personally selected, she told me, by Isaac Breitzen. Monty's file was not one of those. Monty's record was pretty good, I remembered, but it was a record distinguished by simple loyalty and endurance more than any one thing spectacular. A couple of faint-praise letters of customer commendation that frankly made me wonder whether they hadn't been solicited: *We wish to acknowledge his competence* was the phrase that set me to thinking. Look at his file unsympathetically—and maybe I did just that without even knowing—Monty would seem a better candidate for a Sunday school attendance award than anything you'd give for "distinguished service." In the end, I recommended the award go to Clevie Walters, a part-time kid who'd thwarted a B&E while on night duty outside an orthodontist's office in Whitehaven. Played it by the book, Clevie did, crouched behind a BFI bin a parking lot away and called it in by radio. Call me cynical, but I knew that whole "corporate image management" thing—don't blame me, it's Breitzen's term—was part of my job and I figured it couldn't hurt that he was a clean-cut, good-looking black kid. The kind who makes your ash-blonde East Memphis doctors' wives say, *See? There's a good one. I find some of them quite*—and catch herself. Maybe Clevie was even the kind who makes your doctor-wife blush a tad when he walks with a friend, laughing, past the wrought-iron rail outside a sidewalk café, or looks up from a rack in Eddie Bauer. And, image-wise, it sure didn't hurt that the kid maintained a four-oh GPA at LeMoyne Owen College by day. He photographed with the kind of student council president good looks that, for one night anyway, made us the very model of the moral corporate citizen on the *Channel 5 MidSouth News*. I made myself feel good by convincing Breitzen we should throw in his last year's tuition, with a matching grant to LeMoyne. In the end, I'd put Monty's file aside after noting no more than that he was one of the old reliables. Anyway, I told Jimmy I'd go in to the office myself that afternoon, pull the file for him and leave a copy at the front desk, if I wasn't going to hang around myself.

"Good," he said. "Give me a chance to look at it before the boy wonder does."

Jimmy looked at me. "It's not my case, Jack," he said, holding up his hands. "MacDonald has my old shift, now that I've been promoted. I'm just supposed to be . . . looking on. I'm on—" He glanced at his shoes. "I'm on a special project for the chief. A kind of 'consulting' job, you might say." Jimmy smiled, and I knew better than to ask. "You know the man?" he asked me, hinting. "Next of kin . . . "

"Just well enough to go myself." Jimmy nodded. The sun was full bright now. There was nothing I could do here except stand around, and I figured I'd better get on with it.

I stopped off to splash some water on my face at the Circle K again. I slammed back a half-litre bottle of grapefruit juice (unsweetened) right in the store, and realized I'd gotten astonishingly thirsty standing in that lot waiting for the coroner's people to come. I grabbed a coffee, the biggest they had, cheated them out of the price of the second cardboard cup I slid over the first for insulation, and laced it with a carcinogenic dose of that white non-dairy crap and a continuous pour of sugar that drew a disapproving eye from a morning jogger wearing hundred-dollar shoes and a tight-body yuppie sneer.

Five minutes later I sat in the car outside a tiny, pale blue, sun-warmed clapboard house on a street off Cooper; a birdbath on the front lawn was surrounded with a ring of monkey-grass and some despondent blue flowers I couldn't name. I waited till I saw a light and movement inside. I whispered a prayer I got no answer to and wiped my eyes and wondered: Where does the love of God go in the minutes before you knock on the door in the middle of an old lady's toast and marmalade to tell her that her husband has bled to death in a vacant lot outside an empty factory on an autumn Sunday morning in Memphis?

≈　≈　≈

≈ ≈ ≈

There is laughter in the lounge of the Adam's Mark on Poplar just east of the I-240. This is neither East Memphis nor—there is no name for the part of Memphis that isn't East Memphis, or Germantown, or Cordova. East Memphis is white. Germantown is white. Cordova is white. Wait in the line of cars outside a school at three, if you like to watch petite, pretty blondes, their hips full, forever changed by childbirth, picking up pretty blond children and taking them away in cars . . . There is no name for the part of Memphis that isn't east. The part that isn't east is simply other. It is early afternoon in the lounge of the Adam's Mark Hotel. Two waitresses, one of each hue. Pretty in maroon slit skirts. Two customers. The man is big. Powerful. The woman is small and she is other—there is no name for those of the people of Memphis who are not otherwise clearly labeled. The man laughs. The woman laughs. The man laughs louder. The woman laughs a little quieter. The man orders drinks. The woman says no. The man orders drinks. The man demands music, louder, louder, no, louder—yeah. The man laughs. The man says Hey! The man smiles. The man wants to dance. It is two o'clock in the afternoon of a weekday. No one else is here. The woman looks around at empty seats, imploring.

≈ ≈ ≈

CHAPTER 2

Drive any twenty miles of major road in Memphis and you'll see my wife's name a half dozen times on signs. On lawns of houses, from estates down to shotgun houses. In windows of stores and offices, every size, every social class, from upscale down to Mickey Spillane. Make that East Memphis and you'll see her picture, too. Three, four times, perhaps, but for sure at least once. On the side of a bus stop, most likely on Germantown Road, Poplar, Poplar Pike, Perkins, Quince, Kirby, or Farmington. Lynette Bevins Minyard. The smile. The hair. The number. And the line, always bold, always italic, always a standout, and her motto: *Real Estate. 24 Hours.*

Lynette *Bevins* Minyard, of the Drew, Mississippi Bevinses. Old cotton money out of The Delta, kingpins and belles of every ball from Vicksburg to Clarksdale till Lynette's granddaddy had figured out you could make even more money trading the land than you could trading the cotton it gave, and he'd moved his part of the family to Memphis and bought a mansion on Central and a friendship with Boss Crump during the days when Crump ran Memphis like a legitimized cracker Capone. Lynette says she's moved on, that all the Bevinses have moved on and up from the days and ways of that brittle aristocracy. But that doesn't stop an eighteen-by-twenty-four retouched colour photograph of Lynette's Cotton Carnival coming-out from hanging in our hallway, a gold-lamé bow garnishing the top of a perfectly ridiculous rococo frame. But revenge is *mine,* sayeth Jack: Check the guy she's with in the picture. I checked him out. Discovered the dude is doing eight in a not-very-nice penitentiary in Louisiana, a prison named after a not-very-nice country in central Africa. He went down for one of those tacky old telephone scams—*You've won yourself a car, just send me fifteen hundred bucks for shipping.* His name's *Rudyard,* for pity's sake—serves the redneck bugger right.

Lynette's not one bit less tough than the old birds her father flew with. She wears that smile of hers—all right, that impossible smile—and anyone can see she does things for a Talbot's suit that Talbot's may or may not have intended. Her voice when she talks to me can sound wet-soft as a quiet morning rain in a Mississippi soy field, and if I didn't have a hundred other reasons, I'd love her for that one alone. *And* the woman can gouge your eyes out. Which, frequently, is exactly what my sweet Southern darling will do, taking a particular professional pride in it, more than pleasure, when she's made a deal with an extra little edge for her client, especially when the deal's a big commercial lease or a Park Place-Boardwalk land spec thing, rather than a Bob-and-Betty residential. The bigger the deal, the bigger the pride. But she's fair, and there's no hubris in it.

"Made a sale today," she'll say over dinner, and that's about it. Sometimes she shops to celebrate, but it's never a sequinned dress. It'll be a couple of button-downs for me and a new red rubber plunger for the church kitchen toilet. You'll never see her showing any gloating over the commission, though I can tell you Lynette's more than once made herself single-deal commissions that were bigger than my annual salary at Marksman.

When she bags a big one, she'll flip a double or triple tithe to the church. Half to St. Luke's Methodist in Midtown, where we've never even gone. She's made a kind of a deal with the clerk to keep the donation anonymous but mail out an income-tax receipt. The dollars go to the soup kitchen and the food bank and their project building homes for the working poor. The other half goes to our little church in East Memphis. She'll mail a bunch to her old alma mater—she's an Ole Miss girl, thank you very much, and an Alpha Gam. (Daddy told Lynette that Vanderbilt was snooty, but she wasn't going to stoop to Memphis State.) And more times than I can remember, something like this— a quick couple of hundred ends up in the mailbox of some single mom who could use it and won't mind wondering where it came from, or a kids' camp gets a money order from a name they can't read. Or—the girl is *good*, I told you—some money-spinner, some slippery land speculator finds himself personally supervising delivery of a skid-load of condensed milk, paper towels, and cut green beans in cans from Kroger's to a South Memphis food bank, wondering how the hell somebody got that out of him just by asking.

The first year we were married, Lynette talked me into attending Bealleau Wood Baptist, because that's where her family had always gone since moving up to Memphis from The Delta. It was fine for awhile, and belonging to Belleau Wood meant a nice trip into Midtown once a week. But then the church fathers (its mothers relegated to baking and to what the fathers smilingly call "gracious submission") decided in their august wisdom to move out to the 'burbs. The streets surrounding their couple of Midtown acres were "getting dark," the more brazen among the members were murmuring. So Bealleau Wood bought a square mile of low-lying second-growth willow up where Jackson Levee Road joins the 240. They cashed in a bunch of God's mutual funds and built a great bloody gleaming fortress in a defoliated field, where a church should have been, for their thirty-five thousand of the saved. They clear-cut that forest in an arbitrary square, fenced it all in, and dug and dozed it down to bare fields of fire till it looked like *Khe Sanh* with an architect's touch. And an Olympic-size baptismal font to ensure the elect get the degree of dampness the Lord regards as essential to their election.

Belleau Wood got a whole bunch whiter and nearer my God to thee than Lynette or I cared for, and when we found we'd both picked up the neighbourhood nickname for the place—*Six Flags Over Jesus*—we knew we'd had it as members. So now Cornerstone's our church, over on Brunswick Road off the 64, and we like it. They're small, less white, and more friendly, *and* they don't try to fuck with your head.

That's not the way Miss Lynette would prefer me to put it, of course. Used to, when we first met—that's a Southernism, you understand, starting a sentence with *Used to*, and I hate that. So bloody infectious, Southern speech. When we first met, she'd be horrified by something I'd say. Some Canadian thing. Some expression I'd picked up in the army. So and so is *buggered*. Such and such a business has gone *tits-up*. *Bloody* this and *bloody* that. And, a personal favourite of mine—*since Christ was a corporal.* "Well now, isn't that"—and she'd pause delicately in the middle of the hyper-Southern Dixie Carter she'd put on for the occasion— "colourful." And she'd smile that same smile you see on the glamour shots on the real estate signs and I fell ass-over-teakettle in love with the picture and Guess Who—the girl inside and the damn American Woman (*Get away from me-ee*) and I just couldn't bring myself to go running back to Saskatoon after my year at graduate school. Then Lynette's Southern daddy somehow found him a way to buy me out of the Canadian army without my having to formally resign Her Majesty's commission and then he bought us an insanely elaborate wedding for six hundred and fifty of the well-heeled and a half-dozen threadbare buddies from the English department. The people daddy paid put on a show that embarrassed the living bejesus out of Bud and Doreen Minyard of Melville, Saskatchewan. Then daddy made some phone calls and a green card came in the mail three weeks later, along with a job at fifty-K when fifty-K was really something, and all of that led to all of this, and I walked in

BRADLEY HARRIS

the door feeling decidedly lousy and kissed my wife on the cheek.

"Coffee," she said, finishing her lipstick. She left a blot on a kleenex the same red as the Circle K sign. "You've had coffee." There was a hint of accusation, like she'd caught a whiff of bourbon, caught me back-sliding.

"Yeah."

"We're about to be late for church, Jack, and you stopped for *coffee?*"

"Twice," I said, mentioning the stop on the way to the scene, and telling her I'd made a pot of coffee at Cora Franklin's while waiting for a neighbour lady I'd called who'd agreed to come and give what comfort she could.

"Lord, Jack, that's the second time this year," Lynette said. And it occurred to me only then that Monty's was indeed the second violent on-duty death in the Company within the year. The first was a woman, a minimum-wage security guard we'd parked in front of a Kroger's just off Poplar at Highland, near Memphis State. A warm, windy Friday night, the end of September. Tamara Jean Shepard. Twenty-six. Mother of two. Wife of none. A pretty-plump blue-eyeshadow girl in cheap, non-regulation shoes with worn soles that showed the beginning of a bad outside roll. She was a part-timer attending a cosmetology school. Too damn *nice* for the work, really. Wimpy, if it isn't disrespectful to say such a thing of the dead. But Tamara Jean Shepard, mother of two, said she needed the money, and she needed it with about five *really*'s.

27

The recruiter said okay, and dispatch figured, what the hell, it's a supermarket front sidewalk, bright lights, about twelve feet from a Memphis P.D. zone office . . . what could happen?

Drive-by. Nine-millimeter hollow-point round. Small entry, upper abdomen. Large exit, left lower lumbar region. Most of one kidney and attendant tissue spread over twenty square feet of cinder block wall outside Kroger's, with additional spray on a stack of white PVC patio chairs chained to the wall for security's sake. She probably didn't feel much of anything, the paramedics said. Next day, Kroger's had two packing boys in red aprons and yellow rubber gloves out scrubbing the chairs with Mr. Clean and Clorox, and had the chairs back on sale by early afternoon without so much as a markdown, and Kroger's painted its cinder block wall a pure arctic white with a waist high powder blue stripe running the length of the building.

The first cop on the scene, a rookie named Wiggers, took it for a gang-initiation rite because of the apparent randomness of the thing and because they'd been telling him at roll call every day since he'd joined that gangs were active in the area. Then Jimmy Page showed up and told Wiggers he should have figured a gang doesn't bang off a single round, whooping it up like yahoos and tossing perfectly fingerprinted beer cans out the back of an open-top daddy's-money brand new jeep with a Memphis State Tigers pennant flapping at the end of a ten-foot whip aerial. Nobody we talked to on the scene got the licence number, but a CrimeStoppers tip within an hour of the shooting took them to a frat house on Southern. At Jimmy's invitation, I'd gone along for the ride, just to see. A room upstairs: a white-faced kid in a ball cap, drunk and scared-shaking-shitless, getting a lot of bad legal advice from drunk shitheads in ball caps who all figured they'd be going on to law school. And most of whom, except for the one with the white face, probably would be bagging a law degree—American law schools being the kinds of institutions they are.

Lynette's voice brought me back. She tucked a hand around the back of my neck and pulled me to her. We stood like that a minute and then she said, her hand brushing my cheek, "Get you a nice, warm shower, honey. I've laid your suit out."

"I don't feel like going to church today."

She looked me square-on. "That's why you've got to go," she said without smiling, and she gave me a kiss that started out as simple comfort, drifted somewhere else, and back to simple comfort again.

≈　≈　≈

≈   ≈   ≈

Hot late afternoon fades into night. The breathing carries a rasp and a weighty sighing. Greasy hands on the hasp of a greasy cleaver. Chicken in strips. Chicken fingers. Hundreds and hundreds in stainless steel trays slide into stainless racks, roll into a cooler. No thinking now of the cuteness the term carries—fingers. Wipe a hand on an apron. Wash. Hot water at a stained steel sink, pink, sweet soap in long spurts in the hands. Still, they won't come clean. Close enough is all they ever get. Wet, stinging-red, soaped three times and the grease still hides in the cracks of the hands. Breathing. Door propped open, a cigarette in the doorway, smoke sucked, wheezing, in and held. Blown out, it hangs, white and sullen. The butt tossed in a half-full coffee can by the door. To work again, inside. A sigh. Big hands flick sweat from a neck, run the length of a thong tied in a long loop around the neck, center the knot on the back of the neck. Fat fingers pull the thong, symmetrical, feel inside a shirt for what hangs there. The left foot of a common chicken. Brittle. Desiccated. Invocation to Caribbean gods. A door yanked shut, slammed, locked. The dull hammering of a cleaver, a workingman's sacrifice, more cutting, more trays, faster, till it's done.

≈   ≈   ≈

Chapter 3

Sunday afternoon about one, after church, I went into the office and xeroxed Monty Franklin's personnel file. Twice. Once for the official use of Jimmy Page-slash-Gordo MacDonald. Once, unofficially, for me. MacDonald had already called my voice mail and left a snotty message about being sure he got the *original* file, and the *whole* file, thank you very much, and how he'd be in at three to pick it up. It's *Sunday,* for Christ's sake, I said to the phone. I made sure Jimmy Page had a copy in his hands by two, and that seemed to placate MacDonald for the moment. No more calls, at any rate, and I was still there at three and he didn't show. Cops or not, old man Breitzen would have my hide for letting an original file go to anyone. Once, I'd been handed a court order compelling production of a personnel file. It was just five or six months after I'd started at Marksman, a forgettable name, some forgettable connection to a convenience store robbery ring up near the old airbase in Millington. The cop who served the order just stood there and waited. I asked Arlene to make a copy and keep it when we handed the file over. Before she made the copy, Arlene made a

31

quiet call on the office intercom, and the old man appeared. Breitzen grabbed a phone and made a call downtown—I didn't see or hear to whom—and then the old man just whapped the sheaf of photocopies into the cop's hands. "That's all you need," he said. Paused. "And that's all you're getting." Breitzen wheeled and walked away without so much as waiting to see that he'd been understood. I may not have known then who and what Isaac Breitzen was, but the cop must have: All he said was, "Yes, sir." The old man looked at me. "You didn't know," he said. "But now you do. *Never...*" he said, and walked out. He didn't need to finish the sentence. And I have never once let an original document go anywhere since, no matter who wanted it.

I've never seen my own personnel file. Breitzen keeps it, and the files of anyone labeled *management*—plus a whole lot of other stuff—in a vault in his office. The vault, a walk-in, is big enough, secure enough, belled-and-whistled enough, and frankly so damned overdone, that it would make anyone wonder whether Isaac Breitzen isn't what most of the town says he is: about half insane.

I *do* have an idea, however, how thoroughly I was checked out. Breitzen, it seems, hadn't ever hired anyone who wasn't one hundred per cent red-blooded American. Any ethnic origin would do—he's never played favourites or shown any obvious prejudices there, so far as I can discern. Black, white—didn't matter to Breitzen and he'd brook none of the racial scuffling you'll see elsewhere in Memphis. But you'd

better be a citizen of these here U-knighted States.
There wasn't a green-card on the payroll, till I showed
up. I don't know what made the old man agree to hire
me, except that Lynette's daddy owned, or had control
over whoever owned about half the properties
Marksman protected. And, in fairness to daddy and
to me, it's tough to get better security talent. I'd done
fifteen years in the Canadian army. Started out with 1
PPCLI. (*First Battalion, The Princess Patricia's
Canadian Light Infantry*, Lynette had urged me to
spell it out on my resumé—she said it sounded "won-
derful.") Done tours with Canadian Forces U.N. units
in Cyprus, Egypt, the Golan Heights. M.P. school, the
Royal Marines Mountain Leader course, then C.F.
School of Intelligence. Special Assignments with the
Security Service, Ottawa and Washington. I was on
the list for promotion to major when they invited me
to take a year off and do the course work for a
Master's. "In anything," they said. I'm nuts; I decided
on English, the same major as my BA at Bishop's. But
I had to call it "English/Linguistics," hiding a lot in
the slash, and I had to point out the intelligence connection, and contrive another vague association with
the Department of Criminal Justice, before they
released me for a year at Memphis State, renewable
one more year on request. And I requested. I still
don't know why I picked Memphis—I'd never even
been this far South. But I like the blues, for one thing,
and in the days you could buy LPs for $4.99 I'd
romanticized Beale Street as a miles-long strip of
seamy joints with guys in anonymous dark suits lean-

ing out of windows wailing on tenor saxes. I'd looked at the map and I'd been strangely drawn to the names of the places south of Memphis in Mississippi—Clarksdale, where Tennessee Williams once lived and John Lee Hooker was born, Oxford for William Faulkner, places like Tupelo, Tunica, Alligator, Money, and Yazoo City. Maybe I wanted to be near Elvis, or throw something off the Tallahatchee Bridge, or get near to something else, or away from Lord-knows-what, I don't know. But I do know that, between three interviews over three months, Breitzen or Breitzen's people had called everybody I'd ever worked with, from the U.S. Ranger school in Panama to a happily married woman in St. Catharines who'd once been single and a nurse lieutenant at CFB Petawawa and who'd taken the sting out of a nasty assignment dragging infantry reservists through end-less cycles of two-week summer concentrations. The last interview, he'd had a picture of me. A photograph, an 8 x 10. Colour, no less. A picture I hadn't even seen before. It was me, all right, wearing combats with a PPCLI ascot, a pair of Foster Grant mirror shades, a blue U.N. beret and a smile, and standing with a Sterling Mk IV SMG slung under my shoulder some-where on the green line outside Nicosia. I'd been about to ask Breitzen where he got the pic when he stood up abruptly, slid his glasses into his pocket in a comically careful manner. He put out his hand and said, "You check out, Jack." Told me I'd just started work and handed me a Tennessee Private Investi-gator's licence I didn't know I'd applied for.

Lamont Franklin checked out, too, when I re-read his file that Sunday. We had a copy of his U.S. Army discharge papers, honourable of course, and a bunch more. Solid. Nothing remarkable. Just the kind of guy you could put out, time after time, and he'd follow the procedure, time after time. A commendable line or two in supervisors' six-month reviews. "Stable, reliable, dependable," that sort of thing, but nothing, in his civilian service, for any specific actions. A certificate for a bunch of years' service without a single sick day, then a string of them in '97. Flu, the file said in someone's hasty hand. The usual QSTs—Quarterly Summary Timesheets—and weeklies for the current quarter. I initialed the check sheet Arlene keeps on the file jacket. A Company commandment: You look at a personnel file, you initial and date on the cover. Arlene Cody's AC, TJ for Tammy Jones, the time clerk who'd looked at the file Friday, the day the weekly timesheets go in. And right before mine, in Arlene's hand: IB. He'd been in already, Sunday morning, and left.

≈   ≈   ≈

CHAPTER 4

Monday, two things happened, of note. Thing one, Jimmy Page was at my office before I was, early enough to make us among the first there. Jimmy was standing at the coffee counter in a God-awful green suit getting a lesson from Arlene in how to fit one of those little white plastic cones into one of those little yellow plastic cone-holders so that you can pour one-point-two ounces of coffee into the one and hold it safely by grasping the other. If, that is, you're possessed of unusually small, unusually dexterous fingers. A gadget doubtless designed by the same guy who did those stainless steel teapots for Woolworth's lunch counters—tea all over the bloody arborite, guaranteed. Just as I came within earshot, Jimmy said, in a voice too loud, "Tell you what, I'll just use this one, shall I?" He reached around Arlene to the cupboard above the coffeemaker and grabbed a bloody great white tureen of a cup with JACK emblazoned on its face.

"Hope you don't mind," he said as he sat at my desk, raising the cup as if to propose a toast. I smiled, shook my head, and pried the lid off my latte. "Glad you feel that way," he said, and sipped. "We do go back a ways."

36

"Indeed. So?"

"Your, ah . . . whaddayacallit," he said.

"*File* is the technical term, Jimmy."

"File. Cooper Street. Number 869. Abandoned pie factory."

"Ah," I said, and tossed the client job file down in front of him. "The rules, Jimmy, the rules. No warrant. No lookie. Usual drill. You know how the old man is."

He didn't touch the folder. "No, Jack. How *is* the old man. How are you, for that matter." I didn't hear any question marks.

"Same shit, different day." He laughed. I didn't.

He coughed. "So what's it gonna tell me? What *would* it tell me?"

"*If* you could see it," I said.

"Yeah, sure, Jack. I'll play. *If.*"

"Owners since 1932: Byhalia Bakeries Limited. The place is a pie factory till 1973. County health gets antsy. Over what, I don't know. Something. Deals are cut, it seems to say between the lines. The place stays open another year, the deals run out—that's all guesswork—and the place gets a big yellow sign glued to the wall and padlocks on the doors. November twenty-second, 1973."

"Kennedy. Ten years to the day."

"Should we go for the connection?" I asked.

"A career-maker," Jimmy said. "Massive conspiracy. CIA. Nixon tapes. Iran-Contra—"

"Area 51," I said, adding in. "Aliens in the oval office . . ."

"What else?" Jimmy said, seeming to recoil from the banter.

"Nothing out of the ordinary at first. Byhalia Bakeries keeps a full security contract with us till the factory's cleared out, all the machinery and offices and the last of the personnel gone, then cuts it to occasional patrols. Few months later, Byhalia sells to an unrelated holding company. The holding company tries to make a go with a general warehousing operation. That fails. No contract with us at all during that time, but there's a salesman's notes in the file, a guy trying to sell them another security package. This holding company has the property on the market a long time. A year, year and a half, looks like. Sells it sometime before late 1996 to"—I had to look in the file—"Normandy Investments. Now, Normandy starts a security contract in"—I flipped a couple of pages—"September '96. They contracted with us for an armed man on the premises at all times, twenty-four seven. Normandy asked to pick the personnel individually, by name, from our files. It's unusual, that. Most people take whoever we send and they're happy. If they complain, we listen, we sort it out or send them someone new. I thought Breitzen would go ballistic over a client wanting to hand-pick like that, but he said to go ahead and let them have whoever they wanted."

"They pay their bills—Normandy?"

"Major, I'm afraid that information's a matter of client confidentiality, and without your showing me a subpoena or a court order I'm not at liberty to reveal any information at all related to a client's financial affairs."

"Mr. Breitzen would be proud, I'm sure," Jimmy said.

"May I refill your coffee?"

"Certainly. Thank you. Is it marked, Jack?"

"The second yellow sticky, there."

"Creamer?"

"Lots."

"Sugar?"

"Ditto."

By the time I'd returned, there was a crumpled yellow post-it note on my desk blotter and the file was at my place, facing me, a little tidier than I'd left it.

"They pay promptly, I gather."

"Very."

"Highly unusual—pay in advance. Quarterly."

"Maybe the salesman cut him a deal," I said.

"Mmm," he said. "Good coffee. And thanks for letting me use your cup."

"Not mine," I said. "Belonged to a Jack Fenster. Delivery boy. He worked here a few months. We had to let him go."

"Why's that?" Jimmy said absently.

"Reinvestigated him on a tip," I said. "Found out he was some skinhead piece of crap, a no-fooling, card-carrying, neo-Nazi, racial holy war, ship-em-back-to-Liberia white supremacist."

"I wish he were here now," Jimmy said, and took a long, careful sip. "I'd like to give him back his cup."

Thing *two*, of the two things of note that happened

Monday. On the *Channel 5 News*, just before I switched to *Letterman*, mention of a murder. *This just in . . . late-breaking report . . .* Who invented these phrases, for godsakes? Something about a bus driver, Southern and Walker, near Highland, in the university district. A woman. African-American. Dead on the back of a bus. It happens. I caught the name Ruby just as I clicked, and then Letterman, the gaptooth grin, the tail end of a joke, *Ladies and gentlemen*, the name *Jimmy Hoffa*, and raucous laughter fading to a commercial.

≈ ≈ ≈

≈ ≈ ≈

A rattle of pans in the back of a station wagon. Night insects chatter and rasp, oblivious to the metallic hum of an air conditioner. "You go ahead, honey, it's late." A reaching, a grunting. "G'wan home, now—It's late, you gonna be up with those kids as it is! You did good tonight, girl. Go through and lock the front door, will ya, please. Go on, now!" Lord, I'll never get this out my— "Hey, honey. Honey, 'fore you go . . . if Roland's still in there—see if he's there by the meat-cutter . . . Tell him carry his ass on out back, here. Honey?" Shit.

Reaching inside.

Shoes on gravel.

"I'll help you, sugar."

≈ ≈ ≈

Chapter 5

For the record, Lassiter's dead, twenty-some years now—a pipe bomb, we never knew whose, nobody phoned to take the credit, an off-duty in a cafe on the Gaza Strip. Bob Lassiter was dead and didn't even get his bloody blue UN ribbon for his trouble—DND said a Gaza ribbon required thirty days in the zone and not a minute less, don't bother bitching, they shipped him home in a box to his mom in Thunder Bay, and that was that. But I use his name and put it first. Lassiter Minyard Investigations, the most anonymous listing you can get in the yellow pages, a simple unbold black, no address, a number, no voice mail, a tape. It's not a pretty name. Not in any way a standout or catchy. But putting Lassiter's name first seems to throw people off: Calls never come to Lynette's and my residential number. The calls come to a phone in my study. No more than five or six a week, usually. The phone's just a cheap thing bought off the rack at Walgreen's, with a crummy message tape. That phone in the den is the one thing that Lynette doesn't like, and I won't let go.

I have a P.I. licence, and I use it. Not often, I admit,

other than that Breitzen insists I have one hanging on my office wall. But I use my licence when I want to. Which is, for the most part, not. I am grateful for my job at Marksman, I truly am. Grateful to the Company and grateful, in my way, to Isaac Breitzen. I am grateful no less for Lynette's success and her money—how could I not be? It's let us do things for ourselves, and for a few others here and there, that we couldn't—*I* couldn't—have imagined when home was a 9 x 12 in single officers' quarters. But I need *something*. Of my own. And nothing at the Marksman Group of Companies, *nothing*, is your own so long as Isaac Breitzen is at the helm.

So I take the odd case, privately. I will not do divorce. Not any more. Got nothing against divorce. Want one, get one. But the P.I. work's just too damn tacky. Staking out the Rebel Inn on Lamar and waiting half the night, and pictures in parking lots of middle-aged dipshits with drunken bottle-blondes half their age, and I can't use a camera to save my life anyhow. No process service, no repo, no disability fraud. I won't work for insurance companies whose presidents bag a hundred mil a year, and I won't touch anything for an HMO—where I come from, medical treatment's a right, not a damn business. How I satisfy Lynette is: I won't do private investigative work for money. Her attitude is: It's charity. Mine: I'm not bound to the client, I can quit anytime I feel like it. Or anytime I'm made to feel like quitting. Frankly, I think that's the one part that makes it all palatable for Lynette.

She won't touch the phone, she never gives in to the

temptation to cleanse the tape of some little gem, some story she doesn't want me into, some voice she doesn't like. I will give her that. But she does listen, and she does comment.

It had been two weeks without a call, since the Sunday morning at the pie factory—other than the usual routine crud I just ignore and punt to wherever it is those things go when you press "delete." I'd been to Monty Franklin's funeral, and been pleased that Lynette had showed out of the blue, though she'd had to cancel an appointment. The funeral was a small affair, dwarfed by the vastness of the Midtown Catholic church it was held in. Isaac Breitzen hadn't come; oddly, he'd 'asked' me to come 'on the Company's behalf.' As if I wouldn't go on my own hook. As if Breitzen didn't think he owed an appearance.

I'd processed the claim for Monty's pension myself, rather than leave it to office routine, and taken the forms back to the little blue house for his widow to sign. I'd stayed for tea. I'd smiled, and listened to quiet stories. I'd brought a letter of commendation I'd contrived from thin air. Framed. Driven out again to bring her the little collection the guards had taken up amongst themselves. Just over a grand, small bills in a box. And though the company's contribution was a larger, rounder number, I just mailed out the cheque from Breitzen's 'benevolent fund.'

Lynette and I had just been to the usual once-a-month thespian event at the Germantown Community Theatre—a way, way too earnest production of *Death of a Salesman*, with a Biff played by a buffoon who at intervals seemed to wink at someone in the audience. I told Lynette I'd made a sale myself—a new contract with a guy I'd met at a Rotary meeting, a one-man eleven-to-seven night security at a string of cheap leased-out offices he and some doctor-lawyer buddies had built in an abandoned strip mall.

It wasn't until the Thursday after that second week that I heard a damn thing on that phone that interested me. An African-American voice, rich, warm, womanly, sad, angry, scared spitless, and, through all that, commanding. "I'll meet you tomorrow at six o'clock. At Lotte's. You know where it is." Click.

I did know. Exactly. Right on Cooper near Peabody, just a hair south of Union Avenue. What made me wonder was this. The last of about three times I'd stopped in at Lotte's, she'd refused entry to a couple of clean-looking college kids and a third guy out in the shadows behind. The outer door is just a wood-frame screen, but Lotte leaves it latched nights and you have to ring. Lotte's Austrian, the story goes, a promising career in ballet buggered along with a leg crushed in a car wreck, and she's got one of the two kinds of attitude you'd expect to go with the story. Lotte likes the looks of you, you're in. She didn't like the look of the third college kid, the one whose face you couldn't see in the shadow outside the door. *Nigger*, she'd said to herself and any of the few singles and couples in the place who cared to listen. Lynette and I didn't. We paid and left. The voice on my tape *did* belong to an African-American woman, absolutely no doubt about it. And the voice sounded as if it knew all about Lotte.

"I've already written it in your daybook," Lynette said, and she set it by my place at dinner.

≈ ≈ ≈

CHAPTER 6

Jimmy called my private line at eight sharp. Arlene said he'd called five minutes before, and had just hung up when she'd told him I wasn't in yet. "Lunch?" he said, and I said, "Sure. Your turn?"

Applebee's, the north side of Union just west of Cooper, in the middle of a stretch that's prospering, pulled itself out of the tired and gray that is most of Memphis, and has been, I'm told, since a man lay bleeding on the second floor balcony of the Lorraine Motel and a half dozen people pointed to a window up and to the right in a rooming house at $816^{1/2}$ South Main, where the shot had come from.

Decent place, Applebee's. A chain. Decent salads, and one of the few places you'll see blacks and whites in equal numbers and with each other. We'd missed the chance to beat the lunch crowd, but when Jimmy pulled back his suit jacket, tucking his thumbs behind his belt, his badge showed, and we got in right away. It's the kind of town where a businessman needs the police, and doesn't want to mess with them. A badge carries weight, and Jimmy has a way of making it seem a little heavier yet.

I had a spinach salad, Jimmy a chicken caesar and a Rolling Rock. His usual. We'd meet like this maybe once a month, take turns buying. I'd known him about eight years. We'd met at a Toastmasters' club in Midtown, one we'd both joined in some vague hope that the ability to speak at public gatherings would somehow powerfully change our lives. It was a relatively, as they put it in Memphis, 'exclusive' club, and though the members had made efforts, there'd been one too many comments about Jimmy's "charming" manner of speech. I found out fast that what I hadn't already learned about effective communication on the parade square I was learning from Lynette. So the 'Toastmasters' thing had fallen away quickly, and we'd started this instead. A couple of years back I'd found out he was a Rotarian like me, though a different club. We'd rarely see one another in that connection, except when there was a city-wide Rotary event. It seemed odd—both having this case together and being engaged, as we were, in simply furthering our friendship. At least it seemed so to me. Through all those years, we'd only had one other substantive professional involvement—a dead security guard outside a supermarket. So we'd have lunch now and again. Lynette and I would show at the odd cop function. And Jimmy and his always-white, always-babe, whoever-of-the-moment would appear a couple of times a year as Lynette's and my guests at Marksman functions—Christmas, New Year's, Fourth of July, Memphis-in-May. Lord, we even had one for Dead Elvis Week. Breitzen liked the concept of a connection—a 'visible liaison,' he was fond of saying, as if he enjoyed the undercurrent of meaning—between the Marksman Group and the police. He offered to cover the tickets anytime I brought Jimmy to something, or any cop with serious rank. And what the hell—I took him up on it, and put in for the expense. I figured, Jimmy doesn't need to know, and neither does Lynette. That worked till I started to feel tacky and kicked the refund back into the Company's capital-lettered Employee Benevolent Fund. Breitzen's propensity to cling to a phony Woolworth's '50s image of American business never ceases to amuse me.

"Your man Franklin," Jimmy said. "How's his— You know? He have a good . . . you know, pension plan?"

"Career man," I said. "He had his army pension, and the usual range of company benefits."

"Sucks, right?"

"Well, let's just say . . . it's a competitive benefit package. By the standards of the industry." I changed my tune in mid-sentence, decided to let him read whatever he wanted into the euphemism. I didn't get where he was going.

"Life insurance?"

I found the coyness annoying. "What, Jimmy— you think he pulled a knife and slit his own throat for the life insurance?"

"I'm sorry, Jack. It's just—it seems so *senseless*, is all. Guy like that—"

" '*Sense*less,' Jimmy? You're a homicide cop, for Christ's sake. And even though it might be 'senseless' to the rut and run of humanity, it's not exactly a random event, now, is it?"

"Well, Jack, I just wanted you to know that we were still, you know, *on* it."

"I never thought you weren't."

"You're still—Marksman is still . . . "

"What?" I was getting irritated.

"Just a simple question, Jack," he said, retreating into his smile as Jimmy always does.

"The contract's paid, Jimmy," I said. "We're still there, on the property. Armed guards, times two for safety's sake, twenty-four-seven. Just in case."

"They're observing the usual, you know . . . "

"Police lines. Protocols."

"Yeah."

"You oughta know. They tell me you're over there. Or MacDonald. About twice a day."

"We'll be investigating, you know, every angle."

"Including the owners."

"Yes," he said.

"The owners, as you already know—" I said.

"—Are a holding company, yes. And its principals would be . . . "

"A chartered accountant on Park Avenue pays the quarterly payment, as agent for another chartered accountant in—"

"—In Green Bay, Wisconsin," he said. "And the holding company—"

I filled it in for him. "Is in complete violation of Tennessee corporate law by not listing a director in state."

"Yes," he said. "So?"

"We are a security company, Jimmy," I told him, pushing the rest of my salad away. "They own the property. They pay the bills. They ask for a guard. Am I supposed to run a thorough check on the legalities of their corporate registration?" I didn't wait for him to answer. "I have a one-thirty," I said. It was Jimmy's turn to pay, but I just didn't want to play anymore, whatever the game was. I tossed a twenty on the table and walked.

≈ ≈ ≈

CHAPTER 7

Whatever the story at Lotte's bar was going to be, I wanted to see it unfold from the inside, so I got there at five-thirty for my six o'clock appointment, bagged the one seat in the house that lets you see the door—a tiny table, red vinyl chair with its back to a jukebox that played everything from Dorsey to The Dead Kennedys. Patty Loveless railed about your lyin', cheatin', cold dead beatin', two-timin', mean-mistreatin', etcetera. I ordered a coke with a slice of lemon, and read a discarded section of the *Commercial Appeal* while I waited. I paid Lotte with a five dollar bill and waved the change away. Two middle-aged guys—printers, from the looks of their hands—were rolling dice from a leather cup at the counter through what seemed about a four-beer laugh. A dark-roots blonde in blue polyester pants sat at the street end of the bar, her back to me, beside and just around the corner of the bar from a better-dressed woman—Italian, Greek, Turkish, maybe—whom I couldn't see very well. The two of them talked business—a couple of laughs, but mostly just shop talk. Catering, it seemed. Whoever the woman on the phone had been, she wasn't there at Lotte's.

Quarter to six, a woman appeared at the door, hesitated, and smiled. Maroon skirt, matching jacket over her arm, well-tailored. Expensive blouse, straight placket pleats. A European-looking leather briefcase, oxblood, that even Lynette would say was too much. Lotte let her in. The woman smiled again, more broadly, then took the smile back halfway. She looked around. She smiled at me, and the smile felt, for just a half-second, ambiguous. I thought of a poster on my cousin Randy's bedroom wall when we were kids— Marilyn McCoo, from The Fifth Dimension. *Come on and marry me, Bill.* I blushed. I stood. She set her briefcase on the counter, opened it with a practiced flip, pulled out a metal clipboard and a fat gold fountain pen, took down a modest beer order for a local brewery, and got out fast, flipping me a smile on her way out. I was still standing at my table. The blonde, the Italianish woman, the two guys and Lotte all looked. I beat it for the bathroom, trying to make it look as if I were fussing with something at the table just before I headed for the can. When I came out, I realized I hadn't fooled anyone. Even the two guys chuckled as they stood and drained the last dribbles of their beer and left.

The blonde was gone too, by the time I returned. I sat. Across the room, the woman I'd taken for Italian looked straight at me and smiled. She picked up her drink and sipped with a deliberate slowness, walked over to me and stuck out her hand. She wasn't what the crackers call 'high yellow.' Rather, you might describe her complexion as—if you're white and respectably middle-class—*anonymous.* Easily inside the usual range for Caucasian skin. Way inside, it occurred to me, when you consider most folks from India are Caucasian. I've never liked the expression white Southerners apply to light-skinned blacks—that this one or that can 'pass' (as if the alternative were failure). And I don't want to tell you what they say among themselves. Lord, maybe you know, maybe you yourself have an intimate acquaintance—you can't after all, ever really know who you're talking to, who you're telling things to. But if the game was passing for white, which I reckon sometimes for some people it is, she'd bag an A-plus. And what was my game, I wondered, and what grade would I bag? In the then-and-there, she was lovely, and as that fact occurred to me I began to hear the words forming in my head, in my mother's voice: *Lovely* (and my mother's trade-mark pause), *you know, for a—*

Racism runs deep, it runs in all of us, whatever anyone says to deny it, and it ran in me as surprise. She'd said her name twice before it registered. Debra. Debra Gilbert. "Sorry about the—you know—" She nodded to where the blonde had been sitting. "Just a girl from work. I just wanted to see before—"

"I understand," I said. I wasn't sure it was true. I'd done just about enough linguistics with Marv Ching and Guy Bailey at Memphis State, sat half-alert through enough badly delivered papers at the Mississippi Linguistics Conference, to know that this just plain *wasn't*—not a syllable of it, not a vowel—*any*body's African-American vernacular English.

What it was could best be described as a patiently, maybe painfully, certainly fastidiously acquired standard American English. It sounded natural enough, whatever the hell that means. But I was willing to bet it wasn't the dialect she'd grown up with.

Which may be to say: Bryant Gumbel. Which is to say: white.

She pulled a small brass case from her purse and handed me a business card. A catering firm, address on Cooper, just a block away. I recognized the outfit, Food Fascination. The name was a less-than-brilliant marketing move, and the logo was dreadful, but they provided a good product and great service—more than once, they'd catered a function for Marksman, and they were fabulous. Whether it was game hens at a formal dinner or ham hocks and green beans at a barbecue, people couldn't get enough. The card said she was the assistant manager. *Assistant* had been crossed out in ballpoint. I thanked her and slipped the card in my suit jacket pocket.

"Why here?" I said. "Why Lotte's?" I didn't know what to expect. Maybe something defiant, some strange, secret delight: *Because I can get away with it.*

Instead: "Oh, I'd just never been before. I thought it looked like a cute little place, is all." Hadn't a clue, it was clear. When we'd downed our drinks, I suggested a walk. I decided I'd tell Debra nothing about Lotte's ethnic politics.

The evening seemed pleasant enough for a walk. A little breeze had begun to blow, and the thick, wet heat of the day was giving way to a livable cool, though, as

I reminded myself, Southerners know nothing about cool.

We walked north on Cooper. She set the pace—just a sidewalk stroll in the warm, encroaching grey that gradually separates the Memphis days from nights. That stretch of Cooper is a weird amalgam of the incoming and the outgoing, the once-was and the might-be. A successful drum shop and a failing self-styled *ristorante*. A try-too-hard brass-and-fern feminist bookstore and a kite shop. A junk store full of plaster lawn jockeys and greasy back issues of *Hustler*. Debra seemed interested in the might-be, and she stopped at the window of an upscale antique shop, Suzanne's.

"Exquisite, isn't it," she said and smiled at me expectantly. "What do you think of it, Jack?" she pressed when I hadn't taken the bait. But she was pointing a bit vaguely, and she seemed to be looking at more than one item. She was feeling me out, I knew. And I let her. Suzanne's was a place Lynette and I had been once, a few years before, and where I'd watched Lynette slice and dice the owner, cutting her price on a French ormolu clock down to a quarter of the figure on the tag. When we later looked it up and found we'd still paid twice too much, Lynette just laughed.

Debra laughed at some triviality I'd dashed off. It wasn't very funny—not worth the laugh she'd given it, anyhow. I was tired of playing.

"You're not the voice on the phone," I said.

"Yes, I am, I most certainly—"

"That's not what I meant and you know it."

"Code-switching," she said. "Yeah."

"Yeah." I was surprised she knew the linguist's term, but I shouldn't have been. I decided to be direct. "Why, Debra?"

"Ace in the hole," she said.

"What do you mean?"

"I can. So I do. Sometimes." She paused and said it again, with a bunch less bravado. "Sometimes." The second time she said it Southern, said it black. "There. Better?"

"You're pissed at me."

"Sure, why the hell not? White people don't get pissed? White people don't ever try to be—"

"Hey, hey, hey . . ." I'd backed off, physically. In fact, we'd squared off right there on the sidewalk. "And what the hell do you know about code-switching?"

"I am a *business* woman. I have a college *degree*. In English, as a matter of fact. I know what *code*—"

"Okay. But how'd you know *I'd* know what it is?"

"Checked you out," she said. "With Memphis P.D. With a little help from a friend of my sister's."

"That's twice you've checked me out without my knowing," I said. "Counting your cute trick at Lotte's."

"I didn't *do* anything," she said.

"Well, you—"

"I don't know what was in your head. But whatever you were thinking, mister, *you* were thinking."

"Fair enough."

"Look," she said, hand on hip. Gentler: "Hey, can we start over? Jack? Please?"

"I'm sorry for my part," I began to say.

"Screw it," she said. "Straight. Direct. Okay?"

"Okay. If you say you're sorry for—"

"Gotta have it even, huh?"

"Yeah, Debra. I do."

She never said it. I saw the back of the photo she pulled out of the envelope in her bag, and caught just one edge of the front. Black and white. Eight by ten. She turned it and hung it in front of my face.

"Jesus Christ," I said. Neck ripped open as far around either side as the picture let you see. Blood, solid, still wet on her shirt, still shining. She looked like Debra, only in shreds.

Her voice shook. "Just a dead nigger on the back of a bus." She sniffed. "My sister. Ruby. You find the son of a bitch done it. You find him."

≈ ≈ ≈

Chapter 8

I knew Tuesday there was a special city-wide Rotary luncheon at one of the hotels off Airways, and I knew Jimmy Page would have to be there. He was Mr. Finance for a committee building playgrounds in the projects, and he had a report to present, a report two months late as it was. So I saved the question till Tuesday's luncheon, after I checked a few other things.

Jimmy sat at the head table, at the end near the auditorium door. I ignored the big smile and the Jackie-me-boy and leaned over him, a hand on the table either side of the stack of reports he was fumbling with. "You hadn't told me how he *died.*"

"Huh?"

"How he died, Jimmy. How he bloody well died. The, ah, wound. The . . . *instrument.*"

"Well, shit, man, you could *see.*"

"I saw a lot of blood and a lot of cops."

" 'Severe lacerations to the neck'," he said. "It was right there in the report." And it was. I'd checked. But that was all. That and *Dexter carotid artery severed through, sinister carotid artery severed save for a thin fragment of artery wall.*

59

"I'd assumed it was a knife."

"Well, you know what happens when you ass-yume," he said. He grinned, and held the grin though I didn't return it. I stood back. He looked at me and turned away, seemingly to do nothing in particular.

What Jimmy hadn't told me was: The weapon used was a saw. Most likely, what went under one brand name as a flexi-saw. Campers, outdoorsmen. The people who call themselves 'survivalists.' I'd gone and bought one from a cardboard bin at a surplus store on Summer Avenue. Three ninety-five, plus tax. A plastic bag. Inside, a sheet of instructions and a triple-strand wire rope, sixteen, eighteen inches long, one of whose strands carried sharp, serrated teeth. Two stainless steel rings, one either end. Stick a thumb through each of the rings, pull taut. Back and forth, straight line or bent around a small log as you wish. I'd tried it at home on a twig, then a small branch, then the firewood. Cut your way, lickety split, through a log, four, five, six inches' diameter. Or, turns out, as quickly, a neck.

"Look. Jimmy."

"After the—"

"*Jimmy*—"

"*After*—" Heads turned our way and Jimmy's switching to a whisper didn't make it any more confidential. "*After* the damn meeting, all right?"

I waited. I was angry and the anger had already turned to resentment. The man was my friend, had been my friend for years, notwithstanding our little games-playing meeting over lunch at Applebee's. This wasn't like him. I know a lot about resentment:

Bourbon hasn't a better chaser. When the chairman called on Jimmy to present his report, my resentment rose in my throat. I slipped out to the can to count to ten and say a prayer. It worked, far as it ever does. And not bad this time. I felt myself breathing freely and calmly, and the day was bright and clear. I waited by his car.

"Jimmy, I'm sorry."

"Yeah."

"I just wanted to apolo—"

"Sure, man. No prob."

"It's a weird time, Jimmy, I—"

"Sure. Another time, man, okay?"

I felt it rising inside me again. "God—" I stopped. Breathed. Turned. I looked straight at him over the roof of his car. "Ruby, Jimmy. Ruby Gilbert."

"Jesus Christ," he said. "Who hired you?"

"Debra." He pointed his car key at me, started to say something. He looked away, then back at me.

"Debbie," he said. "Figures. It just freakin' figures." I thought I heard a muttered *bitch* as he got in and started up. I jumped when his tires chirped. He made a right onto Airways without stopping to look for traffic.

≈ ≈ ≈

CHAPTER 9

ccording to the police report, Ruby Gilbert had been found on a Number 3 Night Loop bus, the last one outbound, about 11:35 P.M., right where Southern Avenue becomes Walker, just east of Highland Street. I interviewed the driver, Jerry Lomas, at Luke's Place, Park and Highland, where he's evidently a regular. Luke's is a curiously white working-man's bar right at the edge of the 'hood— Orange Mound. Lomas was agreeable enough, and the price of the interview was the price of his beer. The good news was: He drank generic. The bad news: A dozen cans, and he was already half in the bag when I met him, and he chain-smoked generic cigarettes to boot—something I hadn't guessed from the voice on the phone—lighting them from a Zippo with a practiced flip and a flourish and a lingering cloud of fuel oil in the air when he did it. The Zippo bore a USMC *Semper Fi* crest. A glue-on, not an engraving. My guess: The lighter was generic, too, seven ninety-five at any West Memphis truckstop. A wannabe, I had little doubt, but I figured he was a straight enough guy for what I needed. Curiously fastidious, for a heavy smoker: About every three butts, he'd dump his ash-tray on the way to the can, set it on a table outside the men's room door, and pick it up and wipe it with a paper towel, clean and ready for more, on his return trip to the table. I went the round trip with him, once. His was a beer-drinker's pissing: plentiful, and, I guessed, since I wasn't about to sneak a peek, damn near crystal clear.

Lomas said he'd stopped his bus on Southern Avenue right behind RP Tracks, a college bar on Walker Avenue across from the YMCA, leaving the bus pulled off to the shoulder on the railway side, and gone into Tracks to grab a Coke in a go-cup. No one had been riding the bus this trip out, he said. He'd been inside about five minutes in all before he came out again, walked across the road, and re-boarded his bus. Lomas said he'd fiddled with his seat a minute, adjusting it. Said he'd looked down, more or less incidentally, and a little back. Said he'd heard what sounded like a Coke can, rolling. Said he caught something shining out the corner of his eye. Moving. Sliding toward him on the floor. Liquid, he realized. Lomas figured it was soda from the spilled can, running forward down the grooves in the rubber floor, and he got up and started down the aisle to check it out. He was right about it being liquid.

Then Jerry told me that when he'd walked toward the back, looking at the rows of empty seats and whatever had run toward him on the floor, he saw the woman flop sideways onto the floor in front of the rear seat, the seat that runs across the whole back wall of the bus. What he said about her head I hadn't wanted to hear.

The rest was crap. His reaction. How he felt. How he puked. The time he saw this guy, shotgun wound, under an overpass in Cleveland. And, naturally, the offer to present me—me exclusively, of course—his Theory of the Case.

I asked him whether he'd seen anyone else on the bus. Not that trip, he told me. Said he'd let the last one off inbound before he'd sat at the hospital loop just the east side of Danny Thomas Boulevard, from 10:58 to 11:10. Lomas admitted he'd sat five minutes too long at the hospital loop, and that he and other drivers often did so, on the later night runs. "Else you get ahead of yourself," he said. No one to pick up, no one to drop, he'd start beating nonexistent passengers to bus stops along the way. And it's *just* the kind of time, he said, you've got to figure on an inspector showing up at a checkpoint or somewhere in between. He told me that's why he lingered at Tracks. He often did, he said—no point making it out to the Oak Court Mall end of the run ahead of time. More than a couple of brownie points, he said, there was even some risk to your job if you did.

Lomas had me figured for a 'regular guy,' as he put it, the suit and tie notwithstanding. That and the accumulating beer made him presume a certain complicity he shouldn't have, though maybe he would've cared, had he known, and maybe he wouldn't. About five beers into it, and just about the time I started separating his wheat from his chaff, I started to hear *them people*, then *nigger*, and the usual crap that follows. Including how it's not really a bad term after all. How there's white people can be niggers, too. He started using my name a lot. *Jack, Jack . . . Hey, Jack.* Then it was *fuggin* cops . . . and I heard in his rambling, a repetitive natter I knew was the leading edge of a coming account of pervasive social disorder, massive incompetence, and comprehensive conspiracy.

I had all I needed from Lomas. Before he brought up the Bermuda triangle and the Zapruder film, I figured I'd better offer him a lift home. He didn't hear, and just kept talking. I grasped him by both shoulders and made him look me in the eye. "Jerry," I said. "Jerry. Come on." He stared. Smiled. He declined the ride with a slur. I tried to tuck a ten in his shirt for cab fare, and he brushed it away. I offered it to the bartender but she just waved me off and said, "Nothing to worry about. He does this every night. He walks. Lives around the corner." And she added after I'd already said goodnight and turned away, "He doesn't always make it, though."

≈ ≈ ≈

CHAPTER 10

I drove directly home from seeing Lomas, and Lynette sniffed when I passed her in the kitchen, fully ten feet away. She followed me to the bedroom.

"Yeah, yeah, yeah," I said. "I know. Like a brewery."

"And like an ashtray," she said.

"That, too."

She smiled and slid one arm around me as she took the jacket and hanger out of my hand and tossed the jacket in the corner chair with the rest of the dry cleaning. "Hey, I've only worn that once since I got it back from the—"

She sniffed again. She held back the wince and simply smiled. "I trust this little field trip this evening was work, was it?"

"Yes, ma'am."

"Or are you conducting a tacky but torrid romance with some bottle-blonde cocktail waitress on the side?"

"Tonya the tarbender," I said in my best Foster Brooks.

"Nothing like a little trailer park titillation," she said. "What's Tonya got that I ain't got?"

"Spandex pants and hoop earrings."

"Got that," she said. "And better, as you well know." And I can vouch: She does.

"It's the dark roots got to me first, Lynette."

"Just wait a week, honey. I'll have dark roots, too. What else?"

"She's got . . . chutzpah."

"What's that?"

"It's most commonly defined as the willingness to wear white shoes after Labour Day, darling."

"An outright obscenity," she said. "I won't go that far."

"How far will you go," I said, still in the mood to play.

"Pretty far, for you," she said, and she plopped two file folders down in front of me with a Saran-Wrapped plate piled high with some warmed-over *stuff*— something she'd saved from one of the little finger-food, chafing-dish gatherings they seem to have about twice a week at Lynette's real estate office, some specialty-caterer *pâté de whatever* that wasn't *foie gras* and that I didn't dare call meatloaf. "Here you go," she said. "One. And two."

Folder number one was something I asked Lynette to collect for me, though I could have easily arranged to get the stuff through Marksman Security, using the Company's authorized phone-in account, and I almost did it that way till something told me not to. Anybody can check anything at a county land titles office, just for the asking and given a little basic know-how. Though it rarely matters, you do leave a paper trail when you make those kinds of inquiries, certainly when you take copies, and you leave a trace at some offices when you sign the register, should they make you. The stack in the file seemed to be about twenty or twenty-five xerox sheets of varied sizes and vintages, some of them copies apparently made from microfilm or fiche. Copies of the land titles records since the early seventies on the once-upon-a-time pie factory at 869 Cooper. I flipped through the file casually, and she told me she'd go over it with me in detail the next day. "I think you're gonna find it interesting, but it'll take some explaining," she said.

"And two?" I asked with a larger curiosity, since I hadn't even asked Lynette to get whatever the contents of file number two was going to be. I opened the folder. I was tired. I looked, and I hadn't a clue what I was looking at. A document, that's all I knew. Legal size. I closed my eyes, squeezed, hoping to wash away the last of the smoke and grit from my time with Lomas. I still couldn't make it out. Small print—grey, not really meant to be read.

"Figured I might as well," she said. "While I was checking anyway." I gave her a questioning look. Lynette took it wrong and she started off defensively.

"Lord, Jack, she's—you told me yourself she's—"

"What?" Then I saw. It was the certificate of title for Monty and Cora Franklin's house. A copy of a mortgage—a private mortgage, from the looks of it. Pretty rare beast these days, a private mortgage. At least, it didn't look anything like any of the mortgage documents for Lynette's and my place. Even through the second-rate xeroxing, I could see it wasn't a printed form, but typed—pica, maybe smaller—on a badly worn-out ribbon.

"I felt bad, Jack. For God's sake, that poor woman, she's got . . . *nothing.* So I did a little checking, is all. I just had a hunch, I don't know. And that mortgage— that one there? It's an uninsured mortgage, Jack. It's not FHA, not a bank, it's not even a credit union. Private. You don't see a privately held mortgage very often anymore. I've seen two, maybe three, in all the years I've been doing real estate. And it was uninsured. There was no life insurance on it. No protection. Absolutely nothing. And so she was just . . . *left.*"

I was a soldier, first. Now I do security. I can read or negotiate a contract. But real estate . . . I feel clumsy. "So . . . ?"

"This house, when I'm gone, the life insurance policy on the mortgage pays it off," she said. "Now you take that wee little place Miss Cora's in—"

"How'd you know it's little, Lynette?"

"Well, I mean, the neighbourhood, and all . . . well, anyway, it doesn't mat—"

"It does matter, Lynette. And *what?*"

"Well, I stopped in to see her, Jack. All right?" The question mark was there, but it wasn't a question. Lynette never has been much on *asking* if anything's all right with someone, as long as I've known her. Except when that speak-the-words-only Southern politeness requires it. "I had—you know, on the pretext of a real-tor and all, just a little visit. You know—to ask if she was interested in sel—"

"You picked on that poor woman for a—"

"For a listing? You think I drove in there and visited her to get a *listing*, Jack? I did not. How can you say that? I did not *pick* on her—all I did, *Min*yard . . ." That's genuine anger, from Lynette. It wasn't banter any longer. But her anger was already announced. No need for noise, in the way Lynette does angry, so her voice quieted. "All I did. Was have . . ." She turned and stepped away. Quietly: "Shit." Then: "Tea. All right? We had *tea*, for—"

"Lynette, you've no *business*."

I'm not proud, and I sure as hell wasn't graceful. The argument, conversation, discussion, *incident*, what you will, was one of those things that takes three, four, five minutes, tops. One of those things that seems, *feels* like an hour, and is somehow less composed of words, when you look back on it, than of something unspoken, intangible, and twanging-taut as a piano wire tuned too sharp. It was short, and it ended with Lynette crying her way through a string of words I can recite from experience, rote: *Every time you take a case on your own, Jack . . .* every *time*, and a pause, not for effect but because she doesn't want to say it, and then: *You end up acting like*—It's not the kind of remark that comes naturally to Lynette, and her voice always lowers at the moment of speaking—*an asshole*.

And I said it again. I always end up saying it, not just because it's what I always do when we get like this, but because it's true: *I know. I am. I'm sorry, Lynette.*

The touch on the back of my neck was more about forgiveness than any kind of husband-wife thing. We used to make love to make up, a long time ago, and somehow the mere intensity of it seemed to turn us back inside some Edenic kind of place where resentment stayed outside the garden gate. It worked as long, it seemed, as the intensity of the loving exceeded the intensity of the argument that had gone on before. But we don't do that kind of thing much anymore. I don't know whether the arguments have become more intense or the love less. I slept—kind of—on the couch.

Next morning I learned Lynette had dumped some Kellogg's shares from a dividend-reinvestment plan she wasn't terribly happy with. I learned she had quietly paid off eleven thousand three hundred sixty-two dollars and eighteen cents' worth of remaining mortgage on that little house off Cooper and arranged for the lawyer she'd done it through to accomplish the whole thing in a single day and send the old lady a letter telling her a little white lie about the proceeds from her late husband's life-insured mortgage and announcing he'd shortly be sending her a title certificate on that little blue house off Cooper. Clear title in the name of Cora Mae Franklin. There was no bill from the lawyer, and I didn't guess there would be. Lynette has a way of calling in markers long after the obligation's incurred.

I felt like shit all day. I didn't call Lynette at the office, and I knew better than to send the usual flowers and chocolates Southern men do.

≈ ≈ ≈

CHAPTER 11

Next night, Lynette wasn't cold, exactly. Not explicitly. But she'd developed a sudden interest in forties film noir and had stayed up later than I generally stayed awake. She sat curled up with her big woolly socks and a serious-sized mug of cocoa under a favourite old afghan in an otherwise dark living room filled with the blue light of television. And if she slept anywhere near me she was remarkably unobtrusive and managed to make hospital corners on half a bed when she got up, which must have been well before I did. But she'd thawed enough to make me espresso, and to put her hand on the back of my neck while she poured it, and in a way that, this time, seemed to be something more than just forgiveness. I phoned in happy, so did she, and I got to the office at ten-thirty.

That's normally not a problem, the rare times it occurs, but this time I caught one of *those* looks from Arlene, and I don't mean the indulgent smile. I found out why when I looked at the rack of pink message-pad sheets she'd laid out in a line on my desk.

Jimmy Page. Gordon MacDonald. Jimmy Page again. Gloria Petty, one of our field shift supervisors.

Of all people, Cora Franklin. I thought, folded it, and slipped it into my shirt pocket. Then a pink slip that just said, in Arlene's hand, *Manager—Food Fascination.* Jimmy Page again, twice, no number on either of the slips, which is Arlene's little way of expressing her un-appreciation. "He *said* you'd know the number." And a memo from Breitzen's unapproachably grey-flannelled secretary-renamed-exec-assistant Jennifer Edwards. Had it been a summons to the great one's office, I'd have been there quick as a bunny. But it was a memo, partly folded over, and it looked routine. My mistake: I decided to look at the memo last, do Gloria first, and do the others left to right.

Gloria Petty's as good a shift supervisor as they come. Night shift, Midtown zone. She drives alone in a Bronco, on a schedule known only to the office and her, around to all the sites in her zone. She checks that so-and-so is where so-and-so ought to be, and woebe-tide him if he ain't. Drink on the job: You're dead. Gone. Pack your bags this minute, buster. Asleep at the switch: a whack on the sole of your boot with her nightstick. On the slacker jobs, Gloria will take an indulgent view of a little dozing, as long as it's a two-person venture and one of them's a hundred percent vertical. A part-timer, a college kid paying tuition watching an office-building after-hours desk—go ahead and crack a book, but you make bloody sure you keep an eye on those closed-circuit screens: If she sneaks up on you, you've had it. There's not a guard we have who'd be dumb enough to cross her—we do, I admit it, have some dumb ones—and not a good one she wouldn't defend, anytime or anywhere. But she's moody. Cheeriness, I'd learned, was often a good gambit. I called her cell phone. "Yo. Gloria. Jack. 'S up?"

She got straight to it. "Jack, I'd like you to ride with me one night this week."

"Sure, but—" Ride-alongs were a promise I had made to all the shift supervisors a long time ago. Sometimes they ask me to do one. Mostly, I ask them. Either way, I learned, and everybody knows: You can't trust a colonel who won't get his boots dirty.

"Whenever, Jack." She sounded hurried. "You know—anytime. Whenever, no rush, just whenever you—"

"Gloria . . . " What the hell was that about? Her tone had changed before I could ask, as if she'd been within earshot of someone who'd just left.

"Jack?"

"Yeah?"

"Tonight, Jack. It's got to be tonight. Promise me."

I said okay, then she told me she was just pulling into a job site off Summer, and killed the connection.

Jimmy Page was out. I left a message with someone who seemed none too happy to be taking Jimmy's messages. I looked after some routine crap Arlene tried to pass off as urgent. Two job offers of a kind she usually signs for me, proofs of a Company newsletter I had a week and a half to look at, and a draft memo on rules for contributing to the Christmas Club. That's her brand of insolence, but she's too deft and too smooth about it to be called on it. I called Jimmy Page again fifteen minutes later, left another message, thinking:

Jerk—Why the hell shouldn't I . . . Made a mental note to myself, only half-sarcastic, that I should meditate more on the subject of resentment—*cunning, baffling, powerful*—and I called Cora Franklin.

Four rings. Not a surprise, but a little eerie nonetheless—the tape still played Monty's voice. Friendly. Stronger, younger, more confident than I remembered the man. *Neither of us can come to the phone right now* . . . Maybe she was too sentimental to erase him, maybe a male voice on the tape felt to Cora like protection, maybe she just hadn't thought of it. I left a routine message. I was getting nowhere.

I did manage to reach Lieutenant MacDonald. His tone was different, this time. Quieter. Neutral's about the only term I can think of for it. That and a little— strange for a cop—*timid*. He'd been calling, of all things, he said, to invite me to lunch. But it was lunchtime already. We made a date for "tomorrow, eleven-thirty, to beat the crowds." MacDonald suggested one of my favourites—Landry's Fish House, downtown on the bluff overlooking the river. I've always liked to get there early and watch the towboats shoving mile-long barge trains upstream against the current, barely moving. I was, if nothing else, curious to hear what prompted MacDonald's apparent change of heart. I hung up just in time to see my office door flung open, the doorknob thumping the rubber bumper on the wall. Jimmy Page. A grin.

"Well," I said, and motioned him to sit. Arlene?

75

Coffee? Please? For the gentleman." The sarcasm amid all the flourish was hardly lost on him.

"Look," he said. "I just wanted to . . . I just wanted to come clean, is all. The other day, I acted like—I must have seemed to be acting like . . ."

I let it hang a second. "You did. Act like . . ."

"I did." He nodded. He grinned. "Kiss and make up?"

"How would I know where those lips had been?" We'd used the lines before. The tone was different. "Show me," I said.

"The murder weapon," he said. He tossed it on my desk. Plastic packet, stapled cardboard fold-over at the top. Coghlan's was the brand name—the name was common in every store that carried *outdoor*, hunting or camping supplies, from the upscale places to Sears, to the surplus stores, to mail order catalogues, to half a dozen sites on the Internet. Inside the bag, eighteen inches of wire saw, two stainless steel rings at either end. "The murder weapon," he said. "Or an exact facsimile thereof."

"Down to the brand name?" I said.

"Yup," he said.

"How?"

"It's a matter of the teeth. Tooth shape, tooth size, in fact it was right down to the shape of the bevel. The medical examiner was able to match from half a dozen samples we brought her. Coghlan's fit, and nobody else's brand did.

"How'd they get the match?" I asked.

"Young MacDonald's a genius," Jimmy said. "He

figured, if the cut was so deep, maybe it cut bone, maybe he could get the M.E. to match tooth marks to the actual saw." He changed his tone. "I'm sorry, Jack," he said. "It's just been a weird time, is all. Since my promotion. I haven't got a shift or a division any-more, the Chief just has me—I don't know . . . the Chief likes to call it 'consulting.' It all feels like some kind of . . . free-floating, I don't know. Something. I can't get my teeth into—" He glanced. Wisely passed up the chance to smile at the pun, an accidental one, I was pretty sure. I pushed the packet toward him. "A present," he said and smiled.

"Not an event I want a souvenir of," I said. "Besides . . ." I reached into my top drawer, pulled out the saw I'd bought myself, and tossed it on the desk beside Jimmy's. As luck would have it—but *only* luck—the brand was Coghlan's. It was the only kind the surplus store on Summer had. It was the only kind I'd seen anywhere. I'd seen some at Eddie Bauer's, for $14.95, though a peek under the cardboard flap on the bag said it was distributed by Coghlan's. But I didn't mention that fact to Jimmy.

≈ ≈ ≈

CHAPTER 12

I half-wanted to keep Jimmy in my office, find out what the hell was with him, what was going on, what had gone wrong. Something definitely had taken a dive somewhere, and I half-wanted to get him the hell out. I work for a living, I depend on that job, for self-respect if not for the money. And the feeling with Jimmy had gone not so much sour as just plain weird. I got him out of the office soon enough, with lots of, *That's okay, it's okay* and promises of lunch, slap-on-the-back. I signed some things Arlene brought in, checked on some new hires, and asked for a second look at a report on some new accounts across the river in West Memphis. I didn't know why—I asked Arlene to give me five minutes alone. Absently, I picked up the memo from Breitzen. Addressed, simply, to 'LIST,' it said:

> *The Board of Directors has determined that the potential for conflict of interest exists for those members of supervision and management who hold Tennessee or other state private investigation licenses, whether under the aegis*

of Marksman or otherwise, should the same
operate individually as private investigators after
hours or otherwise in competition or in parallel
with Marksman Security, Marksman Investi-
gations, or other members of the Marksman
Group of Companies. While the Board makes
no accusations hereby, and recognizes that no
actual conflict of interest has necessarily
occurred or is occurring or will necessarily occur,
the Board nonetheless reminds managerial staff
of the potential for such conflict of interest,
reminding all personnel further of the impor-
tance, both for the sake of the Marksman Group
and the sake of such individuals, of maintaining
at all times the appearance, both inwardly and
outwardly, of the absence of conflict of interest
or possible or potential conflict of interest. The
co-operation of all personnel is hereby asked
and expected, and we trust that no further
communication of this nature will be required.

The address block may have said LIST, but it might as
well have had my name alone in inch-high block letters.
And the drafting, godawful as it was and though it bore
Jennifer Edwards' name in the *From* line, was pure
Isaac Breitzen, hot off the dictaphone.

Debra Gilbert called on my private number.
Crying. Sobbing. The words came in chest-heaving
phrases. Freaked. I checked caller-I.D. for the source.
I folded Breitzen's memo, slipped it back under the
phone messages, fed Arlene some crap about some

kind of trouble in the field, and drove out to Food
Fascination on Cooper.

≈ ≈ ≈

CHAPTER 13

Debra Gilbert wasn't a smoker, as far as I'd been able to tell. But she'd made a good start on filling an ashtray in the outer office by the time I got there. She'd bummed a pack of Kools from a guy who stood in a doorway wiping his hands on a stained and greasy towel. He was an immense black man who was introduced to me as Roland, no last name. I recognized him from two or three of the times Debra's outfit had done the catering at Marksman company functions. Those times he'd been in black and bleached white, with the black bolo tie that was Food Fascination's trademark. Today he wore jeans and a rust-stained, bone-white butcher's apron over a white T-shirt, a thong around his neck and tucked inside the shirt. He'd been cutting meat, it was clear. Fat seemed to cling to him, hung about him, and he was breathing hard, wiping his forehead with the back of an arm wet with sweat. From the exertion of his work, from whatever the situation was that hung in the air—I couldn't tell. Debra was calmer, but still a mess. The chubby blonde I'd seen at Lotte's was lighting Debra's cigarettes, handing her cups of sugary coffee. Roland was made of sterner stuff, but he still looked shaken. "M'on out back," he said, and nodded me through the office door into the big preparation room at the rear, filled with tables, shelves, butcher-blocks, trays on racks, and plastic garbage pails. Roland led the way, surprisingly fast but wheezing as he walked, every step of the way. "Better watch yourself," he said as we passed a table where he'd been cutting with an odd, crescent-shaped wood-handled knife that looked for all the world like an Inuit ulu.

I don't like it at the best of times, but on that table was more liver than I'd ever seen at one time. He rounded a corner, the floor greasy with I didn't want to know what. He stopped at the rear door, which had been propped open a crack to let in a line of sun. "Okay," he said to himself as if to gather his courage. More slowly now, quietly, he pushed the door wide open and propped it there with the back of a torn red vinyl kitchen chair tucked under the door's push-bar, its rear feet in the gravel of the lot behind the building. Ten feet straight ahead, a wood fence, alternating in-and-out vertical slats, unpainted and weathered, but solid, intact, a good nine or ten feet high. A double swinging gate. Inside, a large commercial garbage disposal bin. BFI. Roland breathed and held. He squeezed between the bin and the fence with a grunt, shoved the bin aside. Thoughts ricocheted in my head. *Christ, don't tell me*, I thought to myself . . . But there was, thank God, no body.

There was, however, a rusted steel barrel. Larger around than a standard 45-gallon oil drum. A steel lid, equally rusted, with a pouring-hole and what looked like a valve of some kind, jutting above the flat of the lid. The lid seemed just lately pried off and set back on, but it hadn't been hammered back in place. "The barrel had went missing," Roland said. "Debbie ast me to look."

FAT, the barrel said in white on its side, and, larger, as a warning to those who wandered the streets, scavenging, in four-inch letters stencilled in a slash across the barrel's rusted curve: INEDIBLE. Roland picked up a stick, pushed it down three or four inches. What came out wasn't just grease. Atop the surface of the grease was something else. Once it must have floated quietly there, I thought, when the surface had ceased to ripple, forming a small meniscus, from surface tension, where the liquid touched the wall of the barrel; now it had congealed, semi-hardened in a floating crust. Atop the surface of the grease was what seemed about an inch of blood.

I grabbed my cellphone. I started to dial Jerry. Clicked off. Then Gordon MacDonald. That felt better, but I aborted the call. I left the back way, without retracing my steps through the back room and office. I told Roland to tell Debra I'd call her later, for all of them to just sit, and to do nothing else.

≈ ≈ ≈

CHAPTER 14

I called Memphis Area Transit Authority three or four times looking for Jerry Lomas. But getting hold of a MATA driver is like trying to catch a MATA bus. They're both scarce. The personnel department wasn't about to tell me a schedule, though he had told me that, when he worked, it was always night, and always Number 3. I had Lomas's home number, too, but it just rang and rang, no answering machine. Finally I just decided to camp out at Luke's Tavern till he showed. My luck: I'd picked a night he must have been driving. I went in at six and waited till well past eleven. You can only sit and drink so many Cokes in a working-class bar, you can only read so many pages of *Paradise Lost*, without attracting a very distinct kind of attention from the pool players.

The experience was instructive, though. Jerry Lomas showed up half-bombed, lunch pail in hand and in uniform, a good half-hour after the time I knew he had to have his Number 3 back at the barn. And Lomas was not exactly, shall we say, dressed to a standard designed to please the regimental sergeant major of the 1st Battalion, the Princess Patricia's Canadian

Light Infantry. His tie was askew, and his shoes and pant legs showed traces of mud not entirely dried. Though he was drunk and slovenly, he seemed to be known to everyone in the place, and nobody in Luke's Tavern batted an eye at the way he looked.

"Jesus, I knew it," he slurred, breaking into a laugh as he stood there, gesturing widely with his lunch pail. "You're a fuggin transit cop. A transit dick. Hah!" He bought me a beer anyway, paid the bartender in cash, left no tip that I could see, sat back down, and slid the can across the table. I slid it back towards him. I showed Lomas my Marksman corporate I.D. again. And my P.I. licence—that one for the first time. Lomas scarcely looked at the Marksman card. But he spent a long time with the P.I. licence, and crinkled the card with his thumb. He just harrumphed. "That thing looks kinda fake."

"Would a transit cop do this?" I snapped a fresh fifty between my thumb and forefinger. He took it.

"Okay, Jack," he said, half-acceptance, half-challenge. "So whaddaya want?"

I got to it quickly and easily, more thanks to the booze in him already, I'm sure, than to any genius on my part for the science of interrogation. He'd said the last time we'd spoken that he'd stopped on the night Ruby died, as his schedule demanded, at the hospital-district loop, before starting off outbound, then was due to spend time at the Oak Court Mall loop, the eastern end of his run. But Lomas had already admitted to stopping and parking at the roadside on Southern behind Tracks, just east of Highland. He had to have—it was where he'd found Ruby. And I reasoned he'd lose nothing in the admission. Parking there might have been counter to regulations, but a bus driver's got to stop somewhere, sometime. I'd seen a bus or two parked behind Tracks before, a driver glancing quickly either way, looking for traffic and the MATA inspector, before nipping across the road. And I'd seen them do the same adjacent to the Wendy's on Perkins Extended, even though that was just a couple of hundred yards up from the Oak Court Mall stop that served as the assigned MATA waitpoint. It's thirsty work. Drivers need a drink now and then. A Coke. A glass of water. And they'll stop, officially authorized or not, wherever they can get one conveniently. Or free.

Or, it had long since occurred to me, to pee.

I knew I'd have to wait for the whole defence, first. "I drink," he said, "to keep going. It's—" He paused and I just knew the word he was going to use. I'd heard the word at meetings a hundred times, admitted it myself just a couple. "Maintenance." The word connotes a quite particular kind of alcoholic. Not the worst, and not the top of the pecking order, either. I knew the routine. I'd since learned to laugh at the word and the notion. At the absurdity of it. "Maintenance." The unadulterated eighty-proof contrivedness. Businessmen used to do it, back in the sixties and early seventies, back when *a few drinks at lunch* was a phrase you could say with a straight face. Nobody real does noontime martinis anymore. Soldiers still do it, I've no doubt of that, though it's far more likely draft or cheap high-test. An army's about the only employer you can have who'll ask you to drink, give you a place to do it, and then subsidize it with prices no civilian can match. Only the drinking's not at lunch, not till after duty ends for the day, and it's beer for most soldiers, for the amateurs, whiskey for the pros among them, the old hands and the quick learners. Some housewives, for sure—often white wine or vodka, something you can mix with 7-Up or Fresca and pretend. You're not drunk, exactly. Just . . . *maintaining*. There's a hundred euphemisms. *Mellow. Holding. Just right*, you might say to someone like yourself, with a wink and a smile and a great big thumb-and-forefinger Oh. Kay.

"I can handle it," is the next premise in the argument. And, to a certain extent, it's even true. Tolerance. It does build. There is, if you will, a practice effect. It works for a while. You can work, you can drive, you can talk, you can *convince*, seeming clean and sober, where someone else would be visibly bombed. At first, you're convincing others. Then just yourself. Then not even that anymore. Still, you insist on *maintaining*. And on calling it that.

Lomas had maintained the farce a good long time. Toughing it out like a trouper, like a burlesque girl well past it but still gamely doing three shows daily. Bottle in the gym bag, a little winked-at Irish in his thermos at the bus barns. He knows, others know, he knows they know, but who the hell cares as long as nobody says.

Then it gets insane. And desperately, desperately redundant. "Tell ya. Tell ya sumpthin, Jack. I'll put myself up. Put myself up after a few drinks. Whaddever number a drinks ya say. Whaddever. You go ahead, man. Set it up. I mean it. You fuggin set it up, Jacko. Put myself up against any—and I mean *any*. Buddy's. Drivin'. Any. Time." Sits back. Sips. Lets an arm fall. Stabs the air with a finger. The drunk's coda: "Anytime. Anytime. Tell ya that right now."

"Where'd you stop to pee, Jerry?"

"Vacant lot. Peabody and Cooper. Some bushes there."

Across a dark side street, I knew, from Food Fascination.

What I had to figure out now was how he'd killed Ruby and got her across a street and onto a Number 3 bus without a trail of blood.

Drunk as he was, Jerry Lomas gave me a slurred, gratuitous clue just as I was leaving. "They ain't even cleaned up the bus yet. It's still at the barn."

"Thanks."

A flicker of sobriety. "I'm gonna lose my job, huh?"

"Yes. I expect."

"Okay," he said, oddly brightly.

I dropped another twenty on Jerry's table and began to walk away. He seemed not to notice my leaving. But he picked up the twenty. He held it in one hand. Cocked his head and looked at it. Folded it. Smiled at it. Touched the fold with a finger of the other. Stroking it. Petting it. Sweetly. Gently. Gone.

≈　≈　≈

CHAPTER 15

I met Gloria at an all-night restaurant, a second-string Shoney's up in Bartlett. The place was well outside her patrol zone. Miles north, in fact, of anywhere she needed to be during her shift. I'd wondered at the choice of place and time—an hour before the start of her one AM shift. I was fifteen minutes late. She'd already ordered me coffee, and it was cold. I apologized and signaled the waitress for a refill. I ordered us both something to eat. I didn't want anything, but the very notion of English muffins seemed comforting. I didn't know which of us needed the comforting more.

"So you want a ride-along," I said. " It *has* been a while. Is there any particular—"

"Nope," she said. "I want a *follow*-along. Surveillance. Tonight. It's gotta be tonight, Jack. Stay a good ways back, and keep it *real* discreet, okay? I'm pretty sure I'm being followed."

I had brought a copy of Gloria's itinerary. The list of sites she'd be visiting. And a xeroxed map with the routes traced in yellow highlighter. She'd already added to the yellow a red line showing the part of the route over which she thought she'd been followed.

The trouble was, she explained, she couldn't be sure when and where along the route she'd been picked up. She doubted it was when she left the office at the start of her shift. She hadn't become cognizant of anything till the first couple of hours had gone. And, Gloria pointed out, she has to check in at the office, at dispatch and the main gate, about two—Marksman's own on-premises security locations, the main gate and office dispatch, are among the sites she checks on her route. And, when she goes south to her other job sites, she more or less *has* to take North Highland Street going straight south. The stretch of Highland south of Summer was where we figured she'd most likely be picked up if someone was following her.

We stopped off back at the motor pool at Marksman and I traded my own car in for the most anonymous-looking beast I could find in the lot, a Reliant decidedly on the last year or two of its service. It was most of ten years old, but it had the virtue of a certain dullness, and a namelessness of colour. The shade had probably been called *silver smoke* in the brochure, but now you'd only call it *sort of grey.* At the last minute I walked back to my car. I pulled two little green metal shoebox-things out of the trunk. I set up one in Gloria's vehicle, gave her the handset, and showed her how to use it. "This is an AN-PRC-25 set," I told her. "Military frequency. It's illegal. And inaccessible. Keep it out of sight. And keep using the company frequency except when I tell you."

I hung back for the first part of Gloria's shift, waited on a side road and caught her as she turned in the main gate at Marksman. Definitely no one following her, I saw, and she confirmed it. I'd seen a couple of people around the locker room a couple of hours back. Dora Jacques, coming off dispatch, along with her scheduler—I'd acquired a certain sympathy for the guy, and I'd learned quickly to stay away from the jokes—Johnny Cochrane. Emily Yates and Randy Whatsit With the Acne, the new guy, just coming on shift. A couple of regulars just getting off duty, people who preferred to keep a locker and change clothes at the office rather than go to and from the job site directly from home. One was a guy who'd been with us just under a year, Vijay Varadarajan. Good man, intelligent, and somehow he managed to make his security guard uniform look like he'd just strode off a Sandhurst parade square, spit-shone drill boots and all. Definitely worth looking at for promotion, I thought to myself, despite the man's unpronounceable name— we all just called him Veedge. The other was Marla Wilson, an old, old standby. Marla worked a six P.M. to two at the Kroger's on Poplar Avenue where they'd shot Tamara Shepard last year. Barney and Virna were busy cleaning locker rooms, and there were a couple of lights on, apart from the front-desk man's, in the offices. I looked. Seemed they were just lights left on inadvertently as people left the office. No movement that I could see. I asked the desk man to catch the lights on his next round.

I let Gloria roll by me on her way out, and waited five minutes. Nothing. Not a single car. Somebody came out of the Marksman lot behind her, but turned the other way. I knew Gloria's route, so I tried to catch up. I'd asked her to follow her routine as she usually did. The sequence of site visits changed every couple of days—the order, that is, in which she'd go around to her job sites. There's no point having a fixed inspection sequence, else there'll be a sequence of phone calls going round the route like a wave, anticipating her arrival. *Hey, she's just left here—looks like you got about five minutes.* So she mixed up the sequence, one day to the next. But there are only so many ways you can go from here to there. And for some job sites, streets or roads you pretty well had to take to get there.

I followed her south on Highland to Summer Avenue, where she hung a left and nipped into the parking lot outside a CK's coffee shop, pulled up right at the door leaving the flashers on, went in, grabbed a coffee in a go-cup, a copy of the *Memphis Flyer*, and got back in. Gloria sipped a minute while she read the *Flyer* under the overhead light, laughing. (I'd been right in my guess: She liked "News of the Weird.") She doused the cab light, and pulled out onto Summer heading west. I hung well back, just to see who might pull in between me and Gloria. There's an old supermarket on that corner, a Piggly Wiggly, open till eleven. Even a little after closing, it hadn't seemed odd to see a vehicle outside, running. It hadn't registered at all, in fact, till I saw him move. Less than a half minute after Gloria, he pulled out into the traffic on Summer, heading west. A Voyager van. Maroon. Not all *that* suspicious, but I had a hunch. I called Gloria on the superduper mil-spec secret-decoder radio.

"Yeah," she said. "God, this radio's a geezer. Where'd you get it?" She'd told me the van she'd thought had been tailing her was red.

I said, "How about fuchsia?"

"Yeah. Kinda red." I sighed. She heard.

I had her take a left onto Holmes. The van followed. Then a right. The van carried on straight.

"Well," she said. "Guess it ain't him."

"Both guesses wrong," I told her. "Pull into this service station. Park right out front and go inside. Buy something. Spend some time at the counter. Be seen."

"And be safe?" she said into the handset.

"No problem," I said. "I don't think that'll be any problem at all." I drove around the side of the building, pulling up to the air pump. I waited. The van slid in, two banks of pumps out from Gloria's company vehicle.

The driver looked. Then backed up so as not to be seen when Gloria turned and looked out the window. I'd been thinking about moving my Reliant in front of the fuchsia Voyager to block its movement through the pumps. But a guy in a ramshackle El Camino looked after that for me, shut her down, got out and waited a full minute till she finished coughing, and sauntered in like he planned to be a while. A Winnebago hauling a Bronco with a boat on a roof rack pretty effectively brought up the rear.

I walked over and knocked on the Voyager driver's side window. The head turned. Marla Wilson's face turned a shade something quite like fuchsia.

≈ ≈ ≈

CHAPTER 16

I was in at six forty-five, knowing the call Arlene would get at seven when she came in.

"I *sent* Marla Wilson out last night," Breitzen told me.

"I figured, sir." Breitzen likes *sir*, he decided. Likes the Canadian Forces regulation haircut I still keep. Likes the shoes I insist on spit-shining. Likes the accent. At some level, he even likes the directness. "Mind telling me why?"

"Yes," he said. Softening: "Mind my not telling you?"

"Yes," I said, softening some myself.

"I'm sorry," he said, and it sounded real enough. "I should have told you. It's on a need-to-know basis, and I guess I didn't recognize your—"

"So what do I need to know?" I was starting to get snippy and I could feel it.

"You know, Jack, I was beginning to have my suspicions about Gloria," Breitzen said.

"Why? Gloria? I mean—"

"What you may not know is, Gloria was on duty the night Lamont Franklin was killed."

"So?"

"It was Gloria Petty's function, her . . . responsibil-
ity," he said with some emphasis, "to check on
Franklin's job site on Cooper the night he was killed.
It was right on her route sheet. And, what's more." He
sniffed, hesitated. "I asked her to. And she didn't. I
wanted to check—"

"Wait. You're saying you think Monty's death was
some kind of *in*side thing, and—I don't get it. Gloria?"

There was some claptrap about its being a senior
manager's duty to investigate every possibility, consider every conceivable hypothesis and test it, check
every angle, peer into every nook and cranny, there are
times when managerial obligation entails that one's
suspicions must be cast where one would rather not
cast them, most particularly in the security business
and most especially in these trying and perplexing
times, yadda yadda.

I left perplexed. I left understanding only that the
column by the window didn't add up to the one by the
door. I left without saying a bloody thing of any intelligence at all.

I spent an hour, after hours and off premises, with
Gloria Petty. I learned that she'd been sick. That she'd
gone to an all-night medical clinic and had a claim
sheet to prove it—with, as if I'd needed more, a string
of letters over a billing complaint arising from her visit.
That she'd told the dispatcher. That much Breitzen
knew.

I spent twenty minutes driving across town to the
site of an abandoned pie factory at 869 Cooper Street,

arriving in time to watch the third and last battalion of Memphis firefighters arrive, shouting and suffering smoke inhalation and desperately running hose to a flaming lost cause that must have lit the sky all the way to Germantown and beyond.

I spent half the night with my wife and about three pots of some seriously wretched coffee going over the file she'd put together at the county land titles office. I learned that the pie factory on Cooper had been owned for years by a bona fide outfit named Byhalia Bakeries. That Byhalia had sold it to a legitimate holding company based somewhere, owned by so-and-so, I can't remember and it doesn't matter. That this holding company sold to another one, who sold to the one we were working for. That a caveat claiming a right of first refusal to purchase at an absurdly tiny price (tiny, at least, for a recoverable building on land moving up in value) had been filed six months earlier by a company whose sole director was a lawyer upstate in Dyersburg. The lawyer, a local boy at a daddy-owns-it law firm, was acting as Tennessee agent for a Delaware corporation which in turn was owned outright by a numbered Wisconsin company whose sole listed shareholder was a holding company whose sole director was a guy with an address in a mobile home park in Dyersburg ("But it's a real *nice* mobile home park," Lynette told me). The guy seemed to be just a guy—your basic self-employed welder. In fact, according to the corporate records filed with the state government, the guy ran a shop listed in the Yellow Pages under small engine repair and was probably not the sort of guy you'd think would think up a name for a company like Normandy Holdings. Lynette didn't know what the hell to make of it and neither did I, and we went to bed about four and made sleepy love till we were awakened by some of the worst and loudest rap music on record because I'd pressed FM1 instead of FM2 and managed to muff the volume as well. Lynette kissed me at the door as I left, and lovingly whispered the suggestion we spend a sweetly romantic weekend at the Motel 8 (king size vibrating beds, no-smoking rooms on request, complimentary continental breakfast, triple-A off-season rates, shower cap included) in Dyersburg, Tennessee.

≈ ≈ ≈

CHAPTER 17

I have never even once cheated on Lynette. As close as I have come was this. As close as I will ever come is this.

Her name was Mattie, Mattie Catherine Beaton. We'd known one another casually in the last year, year and a half of high school, through a thing we belonged to, a young people's United Nations Association thing, though I went, like everyone else I knew, to Crescent Heights High School and she was president of the student's council at St. Mary's Catholic. They used to hold model UN assemblies for us in the gym at Crescent Heights and Mattie Beaton got to choose to be the distinguished delegate from France and she used to wear a red beret, maybe more maroon, like the Airborne, while I got stuck for a year with serving as the delegate from Jordan and became entirely bored with it except for getting to be near Mattie. I never did get to make a speech in reply to anything Mattie ever said in the general assembly, I never got one of the notes the pages passed from delegate to delegate, and in those days I never thought I'd even think about earning a set of Airborne wings or that there'd some

98

day be a picture of me standing in the middle of the River Jordan with a rifle, wearing wet boots and a blue helmet and a laugh. All I seemed to think about then was Mattie's laugh, the clean, quick way it rang like china teacups. I moved away at the end of the summer that ended high school, had my very first bought-in-a-bar drink the night I got the nerve to call and ask her out. Rum and coke, the very first time I'd ordered a drink in a public place, the night before I caught the plane for Ottawa, and I leaned over and kissed her in the car. I couldn't not, there simply wasn't any way I couldn't. Lord, it was easy and she slid into my arms and her lips were astonishingly supple.

There were letters, there were a couple of strangely reluctant titillating weekends, the conflict of let's-be-friends and I-could-learn-to-love-you, and a long day spent leaning on a rail in the rain on the deck of a ferry winding through the Thousand Islands of the St. Lawrence Seaway. And after that, birthday cards the first year, just Christmas cards after that. A nursing degree and medical school for Mattie, a professorship and more. I finished my BA, told my reserve colonel I was going regular, went to the combat arms school, taught there and wherever they sent me. I learned about the girls who come with the beer at Shilo and Petawawa, Camp Borden, Gagetown and Aldershot, Griesbach Barracks, the hot summer sand in the tank country at Suffield and the cold, unending rain out west at CFB Chilliwack, and the bars in Nicosia.

Lynette thought nothing of the cards, we've always gotten so many, especially Christmas, from so many places. Mostly for Lynette. Or addressed to the two of us in careful, curling feminine hands, which often as not means: meant for Lynette. The last from Mattie had said something about a leave from her professorship, and some stuff in a sighing tone vague enough it didn't register. Then I got a note from a name I barely recognized, a mutual friend of Mattie's and mine who hadn't crossed my mind in years. There were a couple of paragraphs full of apologizing, I'm-sure-you-won't-remember yearbook-camera-club-glee-club stuff, and then the news itself, now old. Not dead, no. Mattie Beaton is still with us, in fact. Still where she used to be, in a way, all those years ago.

But the afternoon after next, a steamy May day here in Memphis, I packed a toque and gloves, a scarf, and a heavy lined leather jacket, all without Lynette's seeing, all while Lynette was at work. Leaving Lynette a note, then phoning when I thought better of it, I caught a plane, stood in a lineup at Canada Customs, rented a car, stood in a freak inch of snow on the unshovelled sidewalk outside the steel-blue bungalow that had belonged to Mattie's parents and later, when her mom died, to her dad. You don't think of doctors getting sick, let alone professors of medicine. The surgery had left a hollow the size of your palm at that part of your forehead you might otherwise set the heel of your hand when you lean on your elbow or rub the skin of your forehead back and forth across the bone. It had been a tumor, she told me, metastasized, and she told me, too, about a dozen-year affair with a married man who sold aluminum siding for a living. I remembered Mattie's maroon beret, reminded her, and I stood with her in the dark of her dead dad's old living room, holding her, half-waltzing her, and we whispered and remembered and listened all night to the little sounds the house made all of its own accord.

I told Lynette I'd been to a friend's funeral.

I think of this now because, a week to the day after the night I first met her, Debra Gilbert appeared in the parking lot outside my office, standing by my car. She said we had to talk, and where she took me was loud and black. She drank, she'd had a few to start with and she kept me by promising me what I needed to know. She talked to me in a scratchy whisper-shout through whiskey and smoke, and she kissed my ear and ran a long red nail down my neck. I decided to tell Lynette, though Debra had passed out in my car and never did tell me what she thought I needed to know.

≈ ≈ ≈

CHAPTER 18

"**M**essages." Arlene was pissed. She walked in, wheeled, and dumped a stack of pink-pad forms. She fiddled with the spring clip holding them together, aligned it, centered it, and dropped the stack disdainfully on my desk blotter. Some with little stickies, yellow and green, hanging off the sides, bearing little closely written addenda, with exclamation points, all in Arlene's crisp hand, black ink. I looked for people in the pile I could afford to ignore. There had to be some of those, and I knew I'd feel better if I looked at those first, just to reassure myself it wasn't an utterly hopeless mess. If there were any messages Arlene was willing to regard as minor, she wasn't presently disposed to say.

Best I could do: I found one from the police. Gordon MacDonald. From this morning. At some point during the morning, Arlene had begun to write their little messages in quotation marks. It was her way of saying: *I am no longer responsible for covering for you, Jack.* The one from MacDonald said, made all the colder by the quotation marks: "Missed lunch."

The pink sheet bearing Cora Franklin's name listed

three or four calls. "All she wanted, Jack . . ." Arlene loves those pauses. ". . . was to say thank you."

There were several others. An uncomfortable bunch, in fact. Things I'd promised and not yet delivered. I made calls. I faked the first one. I stopped. Breathed. Prayed. Told the truth on the next half dozen calls, and made them promises I was dead sure I could keep, deadlines I could undoubtedly make.

I saved Gordon MacDonald's message for last. It wasn't dread so much as a plain God-here-we-go-again dumbness. MacDonald and I hadn't exactly hit it off that first meeting at the pie factory, the morning of Monty's murder. And his messages about what he did and didn't expect to see in the files I left him hadn't added to the warmth in my mental picture of the man. But I had, it occurred, left him tapping his fingers in a restaurant. I called, expecting just to leave a message. To my surprise, he answered the number himself, directly. A cellphone, judging from the sounds in the background. He was in traffic somewhere. My lucky day: I started, a word or two in the most apologetic tone I could muster, and he just trampled right over me.

"Look, I'm really sorry," he said. "And I have absolutely no excuse. None whatsoever." MacDonald was positively babbling. I just listened. "Jack, I wish I could say I had some big piece of police business, but the, ah, simple fact is . . ." He cleared his throat. "I forgot. I just clean forgot, is all."

"Quite all right," I said.

"And worse," he said. "There was something I wanted to talk to you about."

I was grace personified. Cheery. "Gordon, not a problem. Not a problem at all. I do understand. Believe me, I do." And we made a date for the next day, seafood, Anderton's Oyster Bar on Madison, just off Overton Square. I said nothing at all about my own no-show. No reason to that I could see. The Big Book says, after all: Be willing to make amends. And I was. Willing, that is.

And I was on a roll. Next message . . . Arlene broke in. "Jack, get down to the Med, pronto. Take your cell-phone with you. I'll call the room number in to you soon's I have it."

"Christ, Arlene, who is it?" I expected a guard, a car accident, a bad on-the-job injury, a worker's comp thing.

"It's that woman who's been calling. Debra Gilbert. She's . . . they say she's been . . ." Her voice quieted, quickly. It quavered. Arlene had a history of her own, I knew. "Beaten."

≈ ≈ ≈

Chapter 19

Admittance sent me to an upper-floor ward. All the unit clerk would say was, "She ain't up here yet. They send her up, I'll tell you." Past that, the clerk seemed totally put out even to be asked a question. All I wanted to know was the number of the room where they were *going* to put her. "Look," I said as I stood at the counter. Then I softened, trying to reason. I smiled. My eyes followed her as she moved away to another part of her desk to tend to some task that might or might not have been real.

"Answer the nice man's question, now." The voice was quiet, the smile as gentle and forgiving as it was sarcastic, and the badge was Gordon MacDonald's.

"I called you back," he said. "All I wanted was to change our lunch time. Arlene told me where you were."

"Are we on the same page, Gordon?" I said.

He sniffed. He seemed to consider. "My guess is, yeah. We are. I'm pretty sure. I think . . ."

"Same saw?" I said.

He caught the unit clerk's eye. She looked interested, and seemed to tune in as she looked away. He lowered his voice and took me over by a big sunny window, past the clerk's straining to hear. A wing of the floor emptied of patients, construction in progress, bereft of drapes and furniture and entirely open to the sun. "Same saw, both murders," he said. "Same type of saw, at least."

"But?" I knew the answer.

"Same dunnit. Different who."

"Yeah?"

"The M.E. determined Franklin was done by two assailants. The saw was held more or less in a straight line or a vee, around the front of the neck. One pull, and—"

"Ruby had one assailant," I said.

"Saw cord wrapped around," he said, motioning with his hands. "Pulled upward. Couple of times. A big man, *big* man. And way, way more damage to the neck tissues. Carotid artery. The larynx." He shrugged, shook his head.

"And?"

"And I think you know," he said.

"I think I do, too."

The clatter of a gurney interrupted, an orderly and a nurse wheeling someone down the hall, someone they talked *over* rather than to. MacDonald and I both followed them to the room. "Give her some time to get settled, will you," the nurse said as she blocked the door. She made no effort to hide her contempt.

Half an hour later, they let us in, the nurse warning us she'd expect us out again in five. The contempt had softened to something like distaste. Debra was trying to speak, but she was nowhere close to coherent. And a jot shy of anything like real consciousness. And she was a mess. I'd seen the results of beatings like this in Cyprus. Turks beat up a Greek or vice versa, not to rob, not to warn, not to punish, not even for any credible kind of revenge, but just, it seemed, to beat, for the crime of being one or the other on the wrong side of the line. I'd seen the aftermath of incidents there, and also in the Middle East between Palestinians and Israelis. And, a time or two, I was with patrols that had scattered the beaters right in the middle of their work. The most precise term I have for the worst I've seen is an odd one: *empirical.* Experimental. As if the perpetrators just wanted to see how far a human body can be taken in the course of committing—*performing* might be a more accurate word—an assault, to see how far you can take a body, how far it can be broken, or bent, or peeled. Debra hadn't been taken that far. But I'd not have recognized her without being told it was she. Whoever had done it was systematic. Surgical. Symmetrical. Both cheekbones broken. Both collarbones. Snapped the mandible, left and right, the whole jaw displaced. Massive bruising to the underside of the jaw—kicks, most likely. One eye had been covered with a bandage about three inches thick. The region around the other eye was a contused and lacerated mess. There were, in fact, small lacerations everywhere. Mostly minor. Incidental. Most associated with bruises. But numerous. Probably the result of being thrown around a room. Against furniture. Her assailant, it was clear, had been a massively strong individual.

MacDonald ran a finger absently down the row of rings in the half dozen piercings in Debra's left ear. She moaned. He leaned over to look at the right. "Ouch," he said.

"One missing, huh?"

"Gotta hurt."

"Look like it was pulled out?" I asked.

"Yeah," he said. "Wonder why? I mean, I wonder why just *that* one. The other earrings—and some of them are pretty big, no tear-outs, no lacerations, no— the others don't even look like they were pulled at all. I wonder what it was, what kind of an earring it was."

"This." I pulled an earring out of my pocket. Ten-karat gold. Cheap. Or cheap as this kind of thing goes, I'd learned at Marty's Jewelers on Summer. An art nouveau piece, a little gold filigree square strung from an exaggerated gold teardrop, and that hung from a little hoop. "Nice enough," Marty had said, "but low end." A cheap setting. But a nice little ruby. Marty offered me seventy-five and, when I shook my head, a hundred even. He wouldn't go another round.

"Where'd you find it?" MacDonald asked me.

"Food Fascination. Between the back door and the garbage bin. Just incidentally. Poking around. I just . . . I just had a hunch and I wanted to follow it. So I—"

"Kept evidence from the police," he said.

"Only since six o'clock this morning."

MacDonald nodded, held out his hand. "Okay," he said, and I dropped the earring into his palm.

I took her hand. I began to whisper a prayer. MacDonald cleared his throat. "Do that a little louder, will you." When I was done he said a quiet *Amen.*

We walked out together. "Now he knows what he's looking for," said Gordon, tossing the earring in his hand.

I had to ask. "How'd he know he had *anything* to look for?"

"Debra told us about the two earrings. A deathbed gift from the girls' grandmother. One each. One ruby for Debra and—"

"Ruby Ruby," I said absently.

"What?"

"Nothing. Just a song. Just an old song."

"So let me ask you again, how'd he figure out he has *any* earring to look for?"

"We let it leak," MacDonald said. "We let it leak that an earring had gone missing from the body at the time of the killing. Let it leak that we'd become uncertain about the place she'd been killed and that we'd be looking for the earring—"

"You interview Jerry Lomas?" I asked.

"Night of the murder and once after, sure," MacDonald said. "But we didn't *re*-interview him, we didn't find out about the pee break at Peabody and Cooper, till just—"

"I'm glad to know I beat you to something," I said. "Any prints?"

"Not a one," said MacDonald. "And we've been over every square inch of that caterers'."

"How'd he get the body onto the bus?"

"It was dark," he said. "The man was desperate. Deed was done. He panicked. Luck would have it, he got away with it. Lomas was pretty shit-faced, figured he spent about five minutes off in the trees pissing, farting around with his zipper, a good hundred feet from the bus and on the other side of the street from where Page had to bring her—" It was the first time we'd said the name, acknowledged we both knew.

MacDonald stopped at his car, just a row over from mine in the Med lot. "Not that we've got everything figured out," he said. "Like how you get a body across the street and onto a bus." He shook his head. In his incredulity MacDonald seemed to be coming out of his professional self and into a more personal one. "Without any . . ." He quieted his voice again. "Any blood."

There had been some blood, of course. In fact, a massive quantity—enough to flow down the aisle in sufficient volume to attract Lomas' attention. But what had been missing, the crime scene pictures showed, was the spray you'd get had the lacerations been made while she sat on that rear bus seat.

My own theory was simple. "A plastic bag," I said. "A big green garbage bag. Over the head. Tied around the middle."

"Some would *have* to spill," he said.

"Sure. But he got her on the bus. And he knew the bus was empty and, since he got her slumped down in the rear seat, he knew she wouldn't be discovered for a few blocks anyway. He had time to clean up the scene and get out. And we had no reason even to think of the caterers' premises as a crime scene in the first place. You cops didn't. I sure as hell didn't."

"Till Debra," he said.

110

"What was their connection? She never did tell me."

"Two answers to that question," MacDonald said. "Simple answer: There was no connection. Never knew each other."

"And the complicated answer?"

"I'll tell you if you and your wife tell me and Internal Affairs and the FBI what the hell is going on with that pie factory that burned down."

"There's two answers to that question," I said. And smiled.

≈ ≈ ≈

CHAPTER 20

We were to meet at four at the Macaroni Grill. Dumb name, but good Italian food. About as far out on Poplar as you can get and still be in Memphis, the corner of Poplar and Kirby Parkway. Kirby is the boundary between Memphis and Germantown, the end of all the eastbound bus lines but one. Wait at the bus loop and watch. Pretty blondes in white Broncos pick up black maids at nine and drop them off at three or four for the long ride back in to Southaven or Orange Mound or Binghampton. And there's no way MATA can get you out past Kirby by bus after five. Just as well, perhaps. More than once I've seen GeeTown police pull over and stop a black pedestrian. Always polite, your Germantown cop. But cautious. Practical—he knows the reason folks move out this far. Rumour has it some ironically-challenged sweet Junior Leaguer once proposed a city ordinance that would have required Christmas lights to be uniformly white.

We were early for dinner, checked in with the hostess and waited. "His name's MacDonald," I said to Lynette. "But he's black. Just so's you know."

"Uh-huh." She was already into the menu. "What?"

"I told her again. Leaned in, whispering."

"Lord, Jack, will you listen. You are *obsessed*—"

"For the record, I think she's right." The words were rude, considered unto themselves, but the tone wasn't. He introduced himself, took Lynette's hand in a businesslike way, and smiled. Lynette called him Gordon, easily, comfortably. We had some Camparis —soda for me—and small talk.

I ordered lasagna. Lynette looked uncertain. "I recommend the Alfredo," MacDonald said.

"Oh, that's my favourite," she said, and smiled. She liked him. I wasn't yet sure I did, and that felt strange.

I felt better when the dishes had been cleared away and the table wiped, when MacDonald turned and said, looking first at Lynette and then at me, "I thought tonight we'd all just be . . ." He seemed to be searching for the perfect term, and he looked at each of us in turn again. "I mean completely open in every way." Another pause. And: "Shall we?"

And we were. The Macaroni Grill is one of those places where the tablecloths are newsprint and they give you your choice of crayons or markers and they'll refill your coffee forever if you tip them well. And that we did.

"I *am* Homicide," MacDonald said. "But I *used* to be with Internal Affairs. Jimmy knew it and that made him nervous. Internal had been watching him a while, and that 'consultant' thing was just the chief's way of suspending him without suspending him, hoping he'd do something, get a little loose somewhere. He likes the girls, does Jimmy," MacDonald said, and I whispered something to Lynette. MacDonald didn't miss a beat. "What he's whispering to you, Mrs. Minyard," Gordon said, "is that Jimmy likes *white* girls."

I think I blushed. Lynette just smiled and nodded. "Yes."

"It gets a little worse," MacDonald said, and he looked at my wife. "You may want to—"

"My nose is well-powdered, thank you," she said, and looked him straight in the eye.

"And he likes it rough," MacDonald said. "Extremely rough." She looked away from Gordon's gaze.

"It's a *thing*," MacDonald said. "Some people have it, that particular thing, and some don't." He turned to me. "Like you, Jack. You have an obsession—"

I sat back. My face said . . . I don't know what it must have said at that moment.

"You do," MacDonald went on. "Black. White. A black man with a white name."

"I—" I looked back at him. Lynette said, "Yes, you do, honey."

"It's all right," MacDonald said. "We all have a thing. How about you, Lynette. Come on, now—you have a thing?"

"Have *I* got a *thing* . . ." I wasn't sure I liked her joviality, her going along in whatever he was doing.

"Me," MacDonald said. "Now mine's simple."

Lynette was smiling. MacDonald called the waitress over and ordered Irish coffees all around. I couldn't see his face.

"Me. I can't stand Canucks."

"You . . ."

"Don't say it," MacDonald cautioned. "There's a lady present."

I told MacDonald about my sneaking into the lot behind the bus barns, pawing over the inside of the bus for the earring. "That explains it," MacDonald said. "It's what I figured."

"What?"

"Explains why we picked up your prints when we took the second set," he said.

Lynette looked back and forth between us.

Then he told me: "We just leaked the one about the missing earring. Fact is, it was on her when she died. But I want your help, Jack."

"And I want yours."

"To connect the murders?" Lynette asked.

"They're unconnected," Gordon told her. I added: "Except that Jimmy's obsession led him to kill Ruby and he needed to make it look like somebody else did it, and the somebody else was whoever did Monty Franklin."

"So whatcha got?" Gordon asked.

We began. Lynette got out the files, but she didn't need them. I filled in here and there with details, but mostly, she just sketched on the table, two different colours of crayon for two different things, a distinction I didn't quite grasp but that didn't seem to faze Gordon in the least. A who-owns-who tree-diagram of corporations and directors and shareholders and con-nections. I felt like I was in an MBA class. The whole pattern of corporate ownerships, whose name was on what document. The welder we'd met in Dyersburg, director of a whole bunch of companies he didn't know much about. The Dyersburg law offices he'd pointed us to, an Atlanta decorator's work inside a grand old home, and the name, one of about five hundred on a wall of little black plastic plaques containing the names, engraved in white, of corporations for whom the law firm was acting as registered office for the state of Tennessee: Breitzen Investments Limited.

≈   ≈   ≈

Chapter 21

I'd parked my car on a side street, about one o'clock in the morning, just a block south of Food Fascination but well off Cooper so I wouldn't be seen, and I walked along the street to the hedge that ran the east side of Food Fascination's back lot. I tucked myself behind the hedge and waited, as close to noiseless as I could manage, for the best part of an hour.

So little ever happens on a Memphis autumn night. So little in the way of events, that is. One begins to focus on the small things. Sounds more than anything else. The occasional passing car. Gradually, a strange, sure kind of discernment sets in. I began to focus on the differences between the sounds of the cars passing on Cooper. The difference between those passing north to south and south to north. Rubber at high speed. At low. Voices. Black voices. White voices. Laughter from car windows. Two guys walking home from a bar. The break in pace, the click as one stops to light a cigarette. The sharp change from shoe-on-sidewalk to shoe-on-roadway as they cross the street. The scrape of shoe-on-sidewalk again as the voices fade and disappear. And through it all, the insects. A steady alto chirp: crickets. A chorus. Over that, like the sharpening of Christmas-dinner knives, the cynical rasp of occasional cicadas.

Car on the street behind me. Crawling, crunching gravel, chunk by chunk. Lights off. Rolls on just a little farther. Stops. I didn't dare turn or move—my rear wasn't covered. One car door. Open. Close. Quietly. Leather-soled shoes on pavement. Nearer. I stood stock still. In a place like this, in shadows like these, I'd be better to stay still than to duck. I closed my eyes and fought a sudden urge to cough. An urge I wasn't sure was physical. At that point scared might have been too strong a word. On edge would be too weak. Let's make it sound official: *apprehensive.* I closed my eyes and took myself back to first lectures in the art of infantry camouflage. *Shape. Shine. Shadow. Silhouette.* A spotlight filled the whole back lot behind the caterers'—Debra's addition—and it lit me up more than I'd have liked. Still, I decided not to move: A stationary silhouette, visible or not, is a lot less noticeable than a moving one.

Then he was past me and into the lot. I still hadn't seen him. The crunch of footsteps on gravel moved right past me, up a little slope and in the direction of the fence around the BFI bin. He was quiet, I'll give him that. Slow. Steady.

I heard the gate squeak open, squeak shut.

Behind me, not ten yards away, the movement of a car and the speaker-straining pounding of hip-hop too loud for the stereo it was played on. The car slid past me and into the parking lot on the south side of the street, through that and into another lot farther down. Laughter. The splash of glass and liquid on pavement. Laughter again. The rap got turned up a little louder. Insipid stuff. College-kid rap. A too-fuzzy, way-too-simple bass and a too-cute, high-pitched electronic whine for a melody. The kind of sweet, weenie rap a sorority girl would listen to. But fiercely, defiantly loud.

The sound would drown out my own footsteps, and I moved. First, just to the edge of the hedge. I crouched, making sure my face was in shadow. I watched. No movement. He was waiting, checking to gauge the nearness of the car and the rap. Then, a flashlight, behind the shut wooden gate of the garbage stall. I could see the beam, transiting steadily in lateral sweeps. He was careful, had the beam filtered red. I moved, clinging to the shadow of the hedge. I glanced back over my left shoulder. A hundred feet away, across the street in the parking lot, the car, the rap music, laughter. A black voice from the car, loud, bright, distant: *C'mon, yall! Let's get us some beer!* I moved forward again. Edged up to the electrical box set on a pad about twenty feet from the BFI bin and the fence. The flashlight swung, back and forth.

I waited. This was it. Behind, not more than yards away, a car door opened and slammed. More laughter. Louder rap. I moved, made the corner of the fence in three or four seconds, stepping quickly but not running, being sure not to get winded or even close. That near, he'd surely hear my breathing. I slipped around the side, away from the gate in the fence. I wasn't sure,

119

but I thought I heard it swing, or heard the creak of wood, at least. I looked. The gate was partially open, now, the door nearer me open about two feet. I heard what I was sure was the brush of his body against the barrel. He coughed. Muffled. I moved. I was in. I slid along the left side of the BFI bin, the side Roland had taken me along when he'd shown me the fat barrel. He was there, his back to me. He froze.

Lord knows what prompted the high school actor in me but I said, I actually heard myself saying: *Looking for this?* as I held up Debra's ruby earring.

You see someone like Robert Mitchum just grunt when he gets it in the movies, and you start thinking, our whole culture has started thinking: It mustn't be so bad. Well: It's bad. Oh, Lord Jesus Christ Almighty in Heaven does it hurt. I felt my eyes go wide and stay that way, I felt the air in me desperate to get out as if it were afraid to stay inside lest it die in there, then I slumped and heard the shot. *Crack.* I know it couldn't have happened in that order, but that's how it came to me. I took the round in the thigh. I watched it begin to bleed, detached at first, as if the blood were some-one else's, a mere stain on something not my own. Then the pain caught up with the surprise. I could feel exactly where it went in, exactly where it went out, and the straight, searing quarter-inch cable connecting the in and out. I swear I heard what happened to the flesh inside the hole, a kind of ripping, and I swear I heard a tiny splat behind me on the fence as I slipped and sat down hard on my leg, the one that had taken the shot, and I screamed *Jesus Christ.*

A minute later, my own hand was pressing as hard as it could through the folded layers of a bloody white handkerchief stuck with pure, whining fear to my thigh. I was getting my breathing under control, looking at the red spreading across the broad front of Jimmy Page's shirt as he slumped, unconscious but breathing, in the grease beside the barrel where he'd bled Ruby Gilbert like a sacrificial hen. I was playing and replaying in my head the three shots that had come from MacDonald's gun.

"I suppose the handkerchief is pretty much—"

"Pretty much," I managed. "I'll get you a new one."

"Dillard's," he said. "Irish linen. They're expensive." I managed half a laugh. "Let me go turn off that goddamn rap," he said.

"Thanks for the backup, Gordo. I appreciate you being in on this and all. But you didn't say that crap was part of the plan."

"Mel Torme next time, man" he said. "I promise." He started away toward the car, and stopped. "Minyard!" he called without turning.

"Hurry up, MacDonald, this hurts."

"Don't call me Gordo," he said. "It means fat."

≈ ≈ ≈

CHAPTER 22

It's December. I'm still limping a little, more some days than others, but I've pretty much exhausted most of the more likely sources of sympathy. Arlene bundled my office collection of get-well cards in an envelope and handed it to me summarily with a suggestion I might have a place for them in the garage. Cornerstone still has me on the Wednesday night prayer list, but I'm getting lower on the page every week, the inflammatory phrase *gunshot wound* has been replaced with the more ambiguous *recovering*, and I'm down to one line sandwiched between somebody's uncle's shingles and a generic prayer for good grades on college kids' exams and their traveling home for Christmas.

I'm missing Christmas on the prairies. The Christmases I had as a kid. Fat, fuzzy snowflakes that didn't melt before they hit the ground. Snowman snow, shovel-the-rink snow, salt on the sidewalk, and twig-snapping cold. The little china bells you'd get if you waited in line to see Santa at the Hudson's Bay store. Model trains and snowsuits and words like *toboggan* and *toque*, and breath that hangs in the air in crystals and holds to its centre and drifts across a cleaner place than Tennessee will ever be again.

MacDonald says the FBI figures they'll close in on Breitzen in six or eight weeks and that'll be that. The whole Marksman thing will go tits-up and my job with it. I'll have left before that, of course. They've offered me Witness Protection but I said don't be silly, I'd stick it out. The Bureau seemed to think that was all right, that they had Breitzen and all his people pretty much nailed. I found out one thing that ticked me off: My P.I. licence disappears when I quit Marksman. Not that it's that hard to get a replacement, but, Lord, what a guy has to go through to make a living. I'll get a new phone, one with a decent tape thing. I'll set up my office in the house. I'll let Lynette decide on the decor and I'll put the furniture wherever she tells me to. I'll get myself a new listing in the Yellow Pages: *Minyard Lassiter Investigations.* If Lynette-the-wife doesn't go for it, I'll ask Lynette-the-realtor to find me some commercial property after Christmas and just hope she doesn't gouge me too badly on the commission.

Lynette's gone nuts again this year. You can feel the flipping ghost of Burl Ives singing *Holly Jolly Christmas* twenty-four-seven in this house. She has wreaths and bows and pine cones and bells and advent calendars and holly hanging from every rack and rail in the bloody house. She's got *everyone* coming to dinner Christmas Day. Debra Gilbert's coming, and Lynette's worried sick her cooking won't be up to Debra's standards. I've got Debra a gift certificate for dinner at the Peabody. I figured it's perfect for a caterer, but Lynette says it's a dumb gift, a busman's holiday. We'll see. Gordon MacDonald will be here, and I've already wrapped a gift for him—a half-dozen *very* expensive, *definitely-not*-just-J.C. Penney's, white Irish linen handkerchiefs. Monogrammed. Simple, but elegant, say I, though Lynette's reaction was: *Dull.* Later: *Dumb.* Again, we'll see. And if he reacts badly to that, I've got something in reserve. Hey, it's tasteful. Just a little something in recognition of his Scottish heritage, however nominal it be. Lynette's horrified, she told me I have *got* to learn to think twice about the assumptions I make, and the messages I give without intending to, but I said to her: It's always that way with a haggis—you can't possibly know till you've tried it.

≈ ≈ ≈

Bradley Harris is a Canadian living in
Memphis, Tennessee, where he's
employed to think and write about training
in industry. As fictioneer and playwright,
he writes about American life from the
special position of a Canadian: alien, but
able to "pass" among those whose
language and culture he examines. He is
the author of a full-length dramatic play,
Incoming (produced in Memphis and Los
Angeles), and is at work on three other
novels in the Jack Minyard series: *Six
Flags Over Jesus*, *The Midnight Clear*,
and *Water Moccasin. Ruby Ruby* is his
first published novel.